The Aftermath
The Survive Saga, Book 3
Samuel Morris Jr.

Samuel Morris Jr.

Dedication

This book is dedicated to my wife Christina, my children Samiyah and Sammy, my parents Kimberly and Samuel, my siblings Daniel, Noelle, and Zuriel, my family, my friends, and my supporters.

Chapter One

Thirteen-year-old Robert stood alone on an endless plain, warm crimson liquid pooling at his feet and darkness surrounding him. The thick air smelled and tasted like blood.

He had caramel skin and light brown eyes. Robert was five feet three inches tall with a curly black afro. He wore a black shirt, a charcoal jacket with scarlet mandarin letters on the back, and black jeans.

A deafening scream pierced the silence.

He turned to see the neighbors they hadn't saved submerged in the blood, with only their heads visible.

The redhead had porcelain skin and green eyes, while her girlfriend had blue hair with purple highlights and blue eyes.

They died on their backs in the stairwell, reaching for each other with tattooed half-heart hands. The redhead's right and her girlfriend's left.

As they rose from the blood, it covered their bodies. They clasped hands, and their half hearts joined into a whole. Their skin glowed a luminescent blue against the bloody plain, and the crimson liquid burst away from them.

They turned to Robert and pointed at him in unison. "This is your fault. You left us to die. What comes next is your responsibility."

He looked at them both. "Everything happened so fast. We didn't have time to help you."

The Reapers let out a synchronized pulsing roar. "Liar! You didn't save our lives. It's because of you that we perished. You caused your mother's death."

Robert shook his head. "It wasn't my fault. Nobody saw Lex until it was too late. I wanted to rescue you both, but my dad..."

They pulse roared again. "Keep your excuses! We came for one purpose."

The Reapers advanced toward him.

He retreated. "What purpose?"

They continued towards him. "To say you can't stop what comes next."

Robert's gaze locked onto theirs as they drew closer. "What comes next?"

They stepped up to his face, their vacant black eyes level with his. The Reapers bared their sharp teeth in a smile. "Death."

Their skin turned black, and then they vanished. Robert whirled around, searching for them, but they were gone. When he rotated again, thousands of lifeless bodies lay twenty feet away, surrounding him. He heard countless cries for help, and he clamped his hands over his ears.

Corpses began floating to the surface of the blood, creating a smaller ring nearby.

Everyone who had been with him earlier that night now surrounded him.

General Johnson lay in front of him, with Colonel Brian near Isaac on his left, and Emily close to Liam on his right. As he continued to turn, he saw Mateo, Andrea, Sofia, Jess, and his father, James, lying there.

He covered his mouth and dropped to his knees. Tears streamed down his face as he crawled through the blood to his dad. James was a thirty-three-year-old African-American with espresso-brown skin and brown eyes. He stood around five feet eight inches tall, with a low-cut fade, and full facial hair. James wore a blue shirt, a black jacket with a thick cotton collar, and blue jeans.

Robert reached out and touched his father's face, leaving behind a bloody handprint. Blood trickled down James's cheek, dripping through his beard. Robert stared at his hands and trembled.

James sat up, then looked at him. His physique transformed into a Reaper. James' skin turned luminescent blue. His hair fell out, and his cheeks disintegrated, exposing razor-sharp teeth. James' eyes filled with darkness until they were black. His muscles bulged, body fat vanished, and claws extended from his fingers and toes.

Robert scooted back in horror.

James gazed at him with sorrow. "Sorry, Robby."

He leaped into the air and landed on Robert, biting into his neck. His son screamed in agony.

James shook him awake. Robert's eyes snapped open, and he glanced around, his heart pounding. He heard a deep hum from the thrusters while seated in the Hovercopter's last row. Colonel Brian piloted the aircraft over Downtown, with Isaac in the co-pilot's chair beside him.

In the side chairs behind Colonel Brian sat General Johnson.

Liam, Emily, and Jessica sat in the side chairs behind Isaac.

The frigid air from the open door swept through the cabin, chilling the sweat on Robert's forehead as he tried to steady his breathing.

James steadied him with a hand on his shoulder. "Are you okay Rob?"

Robert looked at him, his voice weary. "Sorry Dad. I haven't slept in the past two days."

James nodded. "I know. It feels like we've been running, fighting, and moving for almost forty-eight hours straight. What did you dream about?"

Robert dropped his gaze. "The couple we abandoned in the apartment stairwell. They became Reapers and told me everything is my fault."

James shook his head. "None of this is your responsibility. This is all Mateo's doing."

Robert turned to his dad, his voice low. "They said I left them to die and I'm responsible for what comes next."

James looked in front of him. "You didn't leave them for dead. If anyone did, it was me."

Robert anxiously rubbed his hands together. "The dream felt so real. Why do you think I dreamed about them?"

James shrugged. "I don't know. Sometimes our minds project guilt into our dreams. But let me be clear, the only person responsible for what comes next is Mateo."

Robert sighed. "Why didn't we try to save them? We should've at least tried."

James turned to look at his son. "In hindsight, you're right. We should have. I wish we'd saved one of them. We didn't know about the Taken and what was going on at that time. My priority was protecting you. I couldn't risk either of our lives. In that moment, I made the choice I thought best."

Robert shook his head. "We rescued Sofia."

James faced forward again. "That was different. The Reapers weren't breathing down Sofia's neck. At the same time, you're right. Maybe we could've done more."

Robert turned to his father. "If you had another chance to choose, would you make the same choice?"

James nodded without hesitation. "If it meant protecting you, yes. You will always be my priority."

Robert managed a faint smile, but it faded. "They said I was to blame for Mom dying."

James frowned. "That was nobody's fault but Lex's. In life and death, he brought your mother down below her potential. You had nothing to do with it."

He placed a firm hand on Robert's shoulder. "I wish I'd had my powers then. Even if Liam had his, one of us could've reacted quickly enough to save her."

James looked his child in the eyes. "Don't let unfounded guilt consume you. Grieving is natural, but blaming yourself for things beyond your control isn't."

Robert punched the seat in frustration. "It's not fair that they died, Mom turned, and Mateo's alive. That's not right."

James shook his head. "Wishing someone dead is wrong, even those you feel deserve it. There's a thin line between standing up for justice and becoming what you opposed. Don't let the hate in their heart consume yours."

Robert hesitated, then nodded.

James cleared his throat. "What did they say was coming next?"

Robert stared at him, his voice unsteady. "Death. Then they turned black and disappeared. After that, thousands of lifeless people surrounded me. All of you were dead, too. Then... you turned into a Reaper and you... you... bit me."

James held his son's gaze. "I would never hurt you. You know that, right?"

Robert nodded. "I know, but... what if it's not your choice?"

James moved closer and placed his hand on his child's shoulder. "If a moment ever comes where you must choose between yourself and anyone else, when survival is at stake, promise me you will always pick yourself. No matter what, or who."

Robert was silent, his jaw tightening.

James pulled him closer, his voice firm. "Give me your word."

"I promise, Dad." Robert mumbled.

James released Robert's shoulder. "Thank you, son."

He veered away and continued flying alongside the Hovercopter.

******

Liam was a thirty-seven-year-old with blue eyes and beige skin. He stood five feet eight inches tall, with brown hair and a full beard. He wore gray jeans, a red shirt, and a chocolate leather jacket with an upturned collar.

He glanced at Emily as she gazed out the window. "I've seen that expression before."

Emily, a thirty-four-year-old woman, had warm ivory skin and striking green eyes flecked with brown near the pupils. She stood five feet eight inches tall, with long brunette hair, and a thin frame. She wore a blue peacoat with a white shirt underneath and light blue jeans.

Emily turned to him, raising an eyebrow. "What look?"

He pointed at her. "That look. When your mind is filled with a million thoughts."

She chuckled. "You think you know me?"

Liam grinned. "I do know you. Better than anyone else on Earth. Would it be arrogant to suggest that I understand you better than you understand yourself?"

Emily shook her head with a smirk. "You're just trying to butter me up."

He gasped in mock offense. "You've caught me! Turns out you know me better than I thought."

They both laughed, easing the tension. Liam leaned forward and rested his palm on her knee. "So, what's on your mind? Why are you staring like that?"

She exhaled a long sigh. "We should all just leave."

He frowned and shook his head. "I wish it were that simple, but we can't."

Emily placed her hand on top of his, her voice soft but insistent. "Why not? Everyone we care about is here. We could let someone else handle this mess."

He covered her hand with his other one, his tone firm but understanding. "We're missing an important person. Sofia isn't here. Plus, who can we count on to step in and save the day? Mr. White's already proven he's not on our side. By the time anyone else shows up, the Taken will be unstoppable. There are millions of people in this county, Emily. No force on Earth can handle that many Taken and Pallid."

Liam met her gaze. "The best chance we've got is forcing Mateo to create a cure or Andrea taking control of all the Taken. Running might work for now, but it's only a short-term solution. I want something permanent, especially after losing so much time when you Houdini'd me."

She punched his arm lightly. "I hate it when you're right. But I see your point."

Emily frowned. "My biggest regret is the two years I wasted being away from you. I'm hoping to make it up to us both."

He rubbed his bicep with a mock frown. "I'm tired of people hitting me. First my dad, then random goon number fourteen, and now you."

Emily laughed, but her smile faded as a bright red glow illuminated her face. Liam's attention shifted to the growing light that stretched from the streets to the heavens.

He leaned out of the Hovercopter and watched in stunned silence as an enormous dome formed, encasing the city beneath it.

He turned back to her. "Well, it looks like leaving isn't an option anymore."

A wave of darkness swept over everything inside the enclosure, except for the glowing Lincoln Tower sign.

The crimson illumination of the dome bathed the metropolis in an eerie glow.

Liam looked at James. "Fly guy, go check it out. See what's happening. We'll land on that building."

James nodded, veering away from the Hovercopter as it descended. Once it touched down, he sped up over the city and suburbs toward the massive red dome wall.

James glanced down as he flew. *'Did I cross state lines into Franklin? That's fifty miles from downtown Allegheny.'* he thought.

Once he reached the dome, James hovered in front of it and stretched out a hand to touch its surface. The dome's energy hurled him back ten feet. He regained control, steadied himself, and noticed that the forcefield's power sources were positioned outside the barrier.

James circled the entire dome and flew to the top. *'There's no way out.'* he thought.

He returned to the group and landed.

Liam turned to him, his expression tense. "How bad is it?"

James shook his head. "Not good. I went around the whole dome. It's about fifty miles in every direction, from the ground to its peak. It's impossible to go through it. The forcefield is like the one surrounding Mateo's lab, but stronger. It repelled me. To make things worse, they've placed the power sources outside the barrier, so we can't destroy them. We're trapped here with the Taken, the Pallid, Mateo, and Mr. White."

Liam snapped his fingers. "Remember all those trucks hauling construction materials out of the city?"

James nodded.

Liam gestured toward the dome. "I'd bet anything they were using those supplies to build this."

He turned to General Johnson and pointed at him with his own cybernetic arm. "Hey, Flattop, what's Mr. White's endgame here?"

The General was a fifty-seven-year-old with alabaster skin and deep brown eyes. At over six feet tall, he had a muscular build, a silver-haired flattop, and was clean-shaven. He also wore winter army camo.

His cybernetic left leg glowed with blue lights along the side, and his matching cybernetic left arm was guarded by Liam.

The General scratched his chin with his right hand. "He's containing the spread. From his perspective, it's better to hold one major city hostage to this threat than risk it spreading across both continents."

Isaac was fifty-five years old, had beige skin tone and brown eyes. He was shorter, with a smooth face, short gray hair, and weighed close to three hundred pounds. Isaac wore a black suit, black tie, and a red dress shirt.

He frowned and pointed toward the buildings bathed in the dome's red glow. "What about the citizens? How are they supposed to escape this nightmare?"

General Johnson turned to him. "They had forty-eight hours to run. If they didn't leave, it's too late. They'll have to survive the aftermath the best they can."

James stared at the General, incredulous. "The best they can? They're defenseless against the Taken and the Pallid. No chance many of them escaped during the worst snowstorm since Snowmageddon. There's no cure for the Taken. If Mateo gets his wish, there will never be. As for the Pallid, we don't even know what they are. Mr. White has sentenced everyone trapped in here to death, including himself."

General Johnson laughed.

James frowned. "I see nothing funny about this."

The General pointed at him. "You're what's funny. You consider Mr. White your enemy, do you not?"

James nodded. "After he tried to kill us all? He's high on my nemesis ranking."

General Johnson tapped his temple. "Then know thy opponent. Mr. White isn't the type of man to sacrifice himself. He will allow everyone around him to die to protect the continents, and the people he cares about. That list is short. It used to be four people, but when I disobeyed him, it dropped to three. And trust me, he's number one."

James narrowed his eyes. "What do you suggest we do?"

Before Johnson could respond, Liam raised the General's cybernetic arm. "James, I don't know if we should believe him."

The General turned his focus on Liam. "If you want to keep your father, Emily, and everyone else safe, you'll listen to me. I have an idea."

Chapter Two

Sofia Hernandez and her mother, Andrea, stepped into the tower. Sofia was a 29-year-old Colombian-American woman with light tan skin and brown eyes. She was five feet one inch tall, with black hair that fell past her shoulders, full lips, and a beauty mark below her left nostril. Sofia wore white jeans and a zipped-up brown hooded leather jacket.

Andrea Hernandez was a fifty-two-year-old woman hailing from Colombia. Her light skin glowed with a dazzling white luminescence, and her eyes were blue green. She stood five feet five inches tall, with a slim-yet-curvy physique and short curly black hair. Andrea wore a white lab coat over an orange blouse and blue jeans.

Their footsteps echoed through the expansive lobby as they made their way toward the GravLift.

Floor-to-ceiling windows stretched from the ground to the second story of the vast open space.

Golden escalators and many Super HD Hologram viewing stations lined the waiting area.

Outside the glass, a sea of red light bathed the city, while inside, the gentle radiance of after-hours lighting cast a warm ambiance.

Sofia glanced at Andrea. "What's happening?"

They walked to one window and gazed at the source of the scarlet glow.

Andrea turned to her daughter. "We must hurry. That can't be something good."

Sofia approached the GravLift. "That looks like the forcefield from Papa's lab. Did you see it there?"

Andrea glanced back out the window. "We never had to use it. The Taken posed no danger to us, since they were under our control."

Sofia raised a finger. "They never threatened you? Not even once?"

Andrea smiled at her daughter. "They were never a threat to either of us. I communicate with them telepathically."

Sofia stopped in her tracks. "You mean you speak to them, and they obey? Or are you implying they talk back to you?"

Andrea held up two fingers. "Both. They adhere to my instructions, and we converse. The Taken see me as one of them. Almost like... their mother."

Sofia's brow furrowed. "Why would they call you their mom? Just because you can interact with them?"

Andrea shook her head. "No. The process your father used to create the Taken stems from what he did to save my life."

She sighed. "When creating the Taken, he used my D.N.A. as the foundation of the formula. They are blood of my blood."

Sofia gasped. "Why did you let him use your blood for something like that?"

Andrea laughed, urging Sofia forward. "Let him? Your father is no longer the man we remember. This version of Mateo doesn't ask for permission. He does what he wants without hesitation."

Sofia remained silent as they stepped into the GravLift.

Moments later, they arrived in the same luxurious hallway they had traveled separately days prior.

Floor-to-ceiling gold-trimmed windows and black marble floors speckled with matching golden accents adorned the corridor.

Andrea shook her head. "He told me he ran my labs to make sure there were no unforeseen complications with the process. Mateo took blood samples daily to check my health. I only discovered what he had done recently."

As they walked, Sofia placed a hand on her mother's shoulder. "I thought Papa might be beyond saving. After what you just told me, I'm certain he is."

Andrea pulled her arm away. "Do not say that about your father. It's still not too late for him. I don't believe the man I fell in love with is gone."

They entered the secretarial area and found chaos.

Someone or something overturned the desk, scattered some chairs, and broke others into pieces.

Sofia pointed at the wreckage. "Papa's creatures did this. They've attacked, killed, or transformed tens of thousands of people into monsters against their will. Maybe even more."

She shook her head, her voice tinged with frustration. "When I agreed to come with you, I held onto a sliver of hope that we could save him."

Sofia let out a dry chuckle. "It's so clear to me now that we can't help him. My goal is to stop him."

Andrea jabbed her finger toward Sofia's face. "You're wrong. If I need to protect your father alone, I shall. You'll see, and when you do, you will thank me for bringing your Papa back."

Without waiting for a response, she turned and strode into Jack Lincoln's office.

Sofia lingered for a moment after entering. She noticed the metal gate above the entryway. "Did Jack Lincoln raise this gate because he saw you two?"

Andrea faced Sofia. "He did. Mateo told him that Mr. White tried to have us killed."

She paused. "Jack said he'd help our family leave the city and get to safety."

Andrea looked at Sofia. "I accepted his offer so we could be together again. Your father was furious with me, which confused Jack. He assumed that was the reason we came."

She looked at the overturned desk chair. "But Mateo said he knew what he'd done. Jack offered to explain, but your dad had a Hunter seize him instead. Jack begged your father to listen, but he refused and had him thrown into the back of a HoverVan at our lab...for later use."

Sofia frowned. "What was he trying to tell Papa?"

Andrea shook her head. "I don't know. Mateo threatened to have his tongue ripped out if he didn't stop talking, so Jack complied."

Sofia's eyes drifted to the surrounding chaos; the broken glass, the overturned steel desk, and the crystal chandelier dangling near the floor. She stooped to pick up a picture frame lying on the marble floor. Turning it over, she found a photograph of Jack Lincoln with her parents.

He was an Asian-American in his thirties with shoulder-length hair, wearing a suit.

She stared at her mother. "It's possible he wasn't a good man. He may have been a monster. But watching someone die like that, just feet in front of me... it was horrifying."

Sofia hesitated, her voice quieter now. "The worst part is knowing my father was responsible. He commanded the Hunter to kill Jack. That blood is on his hands."

The two women exchanged tense glances before Andrea looked away.

She looked back over her shoulder. "Search for any useful items while we are here."

While they searched the office, Sofia turned to her mother. "How do you know he came back here?"

Andrea shook her head. "I'm not. I'm just following my intuition. He and the Taken weren't at the lab. Mateo may have been there before leaving. The laboratory was messy. He no longer has a Hovercopter. The quickest way for him to reach The Agency is via The Web. A tunnel leads straight there, though I'm unsure which one."

Sofia frowned. "What's the probability that he will assault Mr. White?"

Andrea sighed. "The possibility is very high."

Sofia sifted through the scattered papers. "How can you be so confident about his intentions?"

Andrea extended her hand to emphasize her point. "Right now, your father is seeking control. The key danger to that power is Mr. White. He believes that if he eliminates him, he'll be free to evolve both continents into Taken. If he transforms the remaining humans and destroys the Pallid, nothing will stand in his way."

Sofia clenched her fist, a yellow aura igniting around it. "We can stop him."

Andrea shook her head. "I am going to persuade him. It won't come to violence against your dad. You, the others, and Mr. White are all underestimating Mateo. Right now, he's wounded and cornered. Survival instinct isn't so different from animal instinct. Desperation breeds aggression. We don't know what your Papa's been up to since he fled the research campus. That's why we're heading to The Agency. We need to find him and convince him to fix this before Mr. White tries to kill him again."

Sofia stared at her mother. "What if you're wrong? What if Papa didn't go there, and we miss our chance to stop him?"

Andrea looked at her. "What if I'm right this time? What happens if we make it in time to stop him? Besides..."

She pointed to the forcefield outside the building. "He has no choice but to head towards the person who trapped him."

Sofia moved to the window. "He might create more Taken from innocent people. They don't know what's happening, but we do. We have a responsibility to find Papa and stop him."

She glanced behind her. "Why do you think we can stop him with words? After all that he has done? After he abandoned us when we needed him most? What makes you believe the man you loved is still alive inside the monster he's become?"

Andrea walked over to Sofia and placed a hand on her shoulder. "There was this boy named Daniel in my grade back in high school. His father was a major drug kingpin in what used to be Colombia, and Daniel knew it. He acted as if he ran the town. One day, he asked me out, and I declined. When I did, he hit me. Your papa was younger and smaller than Daniel, but he stood up for me and beat him up pretty good."

Sofia frowned. "How does that relate to this?"

Andrea smiled. "Mateo has detested bullies forever. He despises the way they prey on people they think are weak. If we can make him see that he's become what he has always despised, we might halt him in his tracks."

Sofia shook her head. "We must stop him at any cost. What's your plan if he doesn't want to talk? How will you feel if he goes through us to accomplish his goals?"

Andrea stared at her daughter, unwavering. "He won't."

A tear slid down Andrea's face. "We need to save him, at any cost. As your mother, I'm making this decision, and you must abide by it."

Sofia shook her head. "I'll follow it for the time being. When someone I care for is in danger, I will act without hesitation."

She turned away, her voice steady. "You may be my mom, but I'm a grown woman. I couldn't live with myself if something happened to somebody else. Too many have suffered and died already."

Sofia walked toward the GravLift and entered a passcode. She glanced back at her mother. "Let's go. There's nothing here that's of use. We should check The Warehouse."

Andrea typed her code, and the lift powered up. She stepped inside with Sofia, and together they descended.

Chapter Three

Mr. White sat in his dimly lit office behind a sleek black mahogany desk, a cigar resting between his fingers. He was a forty-three-year-old man with praline skin, standing five feet eleven inches tall. His slicked-back black hair and five o'clock shadow framed his sharp features, complemented by his rich brown eyes. He wore an all-black suit paired with a matching black dress shirt and tie.

Smoke hung in the air, curling around the room as the familiar taste lingered in his mouth. To his right, two identical black bookcases stood tall, lined with hardcover books on philosophy and strategy. Across from him, four empty black wooden chairs waited in silence.

Behind the seats, a hologram of Madam President Mary Jackson appeared with sharp clarity.

She was an elegant African-American woman in her early sixties.

The President had chestnut-brown skin.

She stood five feet two inches tall, with shoulder-length black hair and warm brown eyes.

Mary wore a striking red dress adorned with a pearl necklace and matching earrings.

Mr. White took a long drag from his cigar, held it, then exhaled a cloud of smoke. "I'm dealing with my fears."

President Jackson chuckled. "What could a man as terrifying as you fear? You wield terror like a currency to get what you want. Nothing or no one fills you with dread."

He took another deep puff of his cigar and released the smoke. "I worry that Plan Charlie may be too extreme to carry out. The people of this city… I'm afraid we've doomed them. And Plan Delta, I'm worried it won't go as expected."

Mr. White loosened his tie. "Even the best laid plans can fall apart."

President Jackson nodded. "Your apprehension is justified. We plan, and God laughs. I feel the same as you, but I see no alternative except to go ahead as planned. You were the one who convinced me of that. Why the sudden doubt in your convictions?"

Mr. White leaned forward, clasping his hands together. "It's not just the plans that worry me. I'm also concerned about how they'll judge you if the truth comes out. You're the first President in the history of the United Continents of America, a unified North and South America. If they uncover the facts of what's about to happen, it could mean the end of your presidency."

Mary smiled. "It almost sounds like you care about me."

Mr. White returned the smile. "You know you're one of the two people I'm fond of. As my best friend, I don't want you to bear the consequences if my plan fails."

She wagged her finger at him. "Never speak failure into existence. Everything will work out. I'll stick to the story you've prepared. Only us and a few select Agency personnel know the truth."

Mr. White nodded. "I'm going to make sure they're compensated. Money, titles, whatever it takes to secure their complicity. I've also assigned a Watcher to monitor them in case anyone grows a conscience. If they do, we'll handle it."

She smiled at him. "I accept the potential consequences. The well-being of the public is my priority over my historical standing. We're doing this for the greater good."

He rubbed his chin. "Do you think you could carry out Plan Charlie?"

President Jackson crossed her arms. "Are you questioning my ability?"

Mr. White shook his head. "That's not what I'm implying. It's just that... up to now, you've avoided getting involved in the details of what I do, even when it benefits you. You have always kept your hands clean, maintaining plausible deniability. That's how we've operated, and how we've preferred it. Moving forward with this plan will incriminate you and expose you if anyone digs too deep."

She studied his face. "My doubts don't mean I won't do what's necessary. The real question is whether we need Plan Charlie."

They locked eyes, the silence between them stretching.

Mary waved her hand. "Call off the operation. We can't condemn everyone in Allegheny to die. Find another way to end the threats."

He shook his head. "It's no longer a choice to stop it. This city is doomed."

President Jackson jabbed her finger against the desk. "But they're not gone yet."

He held out both hands, his tone grim. "Between the Taken and the Pallid, few humans will still be alive in Allegheny by tomorrow night."

Mr. White folded his hands and leaned forward. "Those creatures don't sleep; all they do is feed. They've been moving and multiplying nonstop for forty-eight hours. While we hunted Mateo and the Taken, the Pallid have been growing their numbers exponentially."

He gestured toward the door. "Even if we assembled multiple units to save the few remaining citizens, it's more likely they, and every soldier we send, would still die. Worse, each service member we lose would become one of them, either a Taken or Pallid. We'd only be strengthening their ranks while weakening our own. It would be a doomed operation."

Mr. White exhaled. "Enough people have died today. If something goes wrong with this plan, you'll need all the soldiers you have left for what comes next."

He stood and leaned over his desk, his tone resolute. "Listen, I've explored all other options. I even tried to recruit the formula thieves, but they refused me. This is the only way."

President Jackson shook her head. "We must try. I owe it to all citizens of the U.C.A. to protect them. That includes the people in Allegheny."

She raised her HoloWatch.

He stretched out his hand, his voice sharp. "Don't make that call. If you do this, you will risk far more lives than you're trying to save. You'll be gambling one billion individuals across two continents for the sake of a few million. While you may not be concerned with your legacy, please consider that canceling this operation could cause you to be remembered as the sole President of both continents."

She lowered her HoloWatch, frowning. "Do you really think I would be the only one?"

He nodded. "Yes, you will. And it won't take years or months. It'll happen in a matter of weeks."

Mary moved away from him and remained silent for a moment. "Are you certain Mateo Hernandez hasn't escaped the perimeter?"

He gave a nod. "No Taken activity or anyone matching Mateo's description has penetrated the boundary. We believe neither he nor any Taken or Pallid has left the area."

President Jackson turned back, her folded hands trembling. "Thank God. Why are you certain he'll visit The Agency?"

He pointed at himself with his thumb. "Mateo blames everything on me."

Mr. White paused. "And he's right to blame me. I didn't stop his experiments. I gave him the resources to create the Taken. By enabling his revenge, I turned him into the bloodthirsty man he has become. I stood by while he tortured the terrorist responsible for the bombing that almost killed his wife. I let Mateo turn him into the first Taken."

He pounded his desk. "I was so consumed with the Evolution formula that I allowed him to get away with things I shouldn't have. His psychological evaluation flagged his instability, but his intelligence was too valuable to ignore. I overlooked my concerns because of his talent. He was a gifted scientist, and I needed that formula."

Mr. White dropped into his chair, his shoulders sagging. "I had so many chances to stop him. My biggest mistake was not killing him myself. I entrusted what turned out to be the most critical task of my career to a regular agent. Oliver, Brian, and I should've handled it. Because of my decisions, we're in this predicament."

He stood, his voice heavy with regret. "I apologize for dropping this mess in your lap."

President Jackson perched on the edge of her desk, her gaze softening. "You know I love you, White. What's done is done. All we have now is the future."

She rose and walked over to her bar, pouring herself a glass of peach Moscato. "How will you fend off Mateo and an army of Taken?"

Mr. White pulled out a bottle of bourbon. "Don't worry about that. I have a secure room. No one gets in until I say so."

Mary returned to her desk. "Are you expecting those formula thieves to pay you a visit as well?"

He dropped two ice cubes into a tumbler and poured the brown liquor. "They'll come for him first, and I expect to be next, after what's about to happen."

Mr. White rubbed his chin. "I hope they do. I have plans for them. They just aren't aware of it yet."

She sipped her wine. "How will you deal with Mateo, the Taken, and the thieves?"

He swirled his amber spirit around the ice cubes. "Never mind me. I have a contingency plan."

They raised their glasses to each other, both taking a drink. Mary took a sip while he downed his glass.

Mr. White slammed the tumbler down. "It's time to start Plan Charlie."

She sighed as she lifted her HoloWatch.

One of Mr. White's agents appeared via hologram over her watch. "Madam President."

She stared at Mr. White. He nodded.

She glanced back at the agent. "Do it."

Then, a red forcefield activated.

Chapter Four

As they stood bathed in the red glow of the forcefield atop a building rooftop, General Johnson held out his hand. "And that's my plan."

Liam threw up his hands. "That's your master plan?"

The General nodded.

Liam pinched the bridge of his nose. "Let me get this straight. You want us to stop searching for the culprit from the last two days and instead join forces with Mr. White at The Agency, hoping Mateo shows up?"

General Johnson turned to Isaac. "Your son isn't a stickler for the details, is he?"

Liam held up a hand. "I'm meticulous with well-developed plans. But when I hear something ridiculous, I analyze it, tear it apart, and confront the person who came up with it."

He sighed. "What makes you suspect Mateo is going to attack Mr. White?"

The General gestured toward the forcefield. "Where would he go besides that?"

James stared at the energy barrier. '*Where else are we headed?*' he thought.

He turned to General Johnson. "How do we know he didn't leave before the forcefield activated?"

Colonel Brian, aged fifty-five, had praline-toned skin and brown eyes. He stood six feet tall, with a muscular physique, a clean-shaven face, and neatly cropped jet-black hair. He wore a winter army camouflage.

The Colonel shook his head. "Mr. White wouldn't trap the citizens in here with those monsters unless it served a purpose. He would only use such drastic measures if he believed Mateo was still contained."

Robert turned to James. "It makes sense. If those trucks were delivering equipment for the forcefield, they must've set it up while we were at the research campus. Mateo couldn't have escaped in time."

Jessica, standing five feet six inches tall with golden-brown skin, light brown almond-shaped eyes, and a mane of curly black hair, wore a purple hoodie paired with dark blue jeans.

She tapped James on the arm. "Don't forget, General Johnson shot him as he fled the campus. That had to slow him down, right?"

The General nodded. "He's still inside the forcefield. Mateo is injured and furious, and his target is at The Agency."

Liam threw his hands into the air. "Even so, this mission is suicide."

Emily shrugged. "If Mateo's already dying, what does he have to lose?"

He shot her a narrow glare. "You're supposed to be on my side."

She met his gaze. "The truth is the truth."

Liam pointed an accusing finger at her. "You just lost your Christmas gift with that betrayal."

He turned to the others, his eyes sweeping across the group. "Even if all seven of you are right, I refuse to join forces with Mr. Shite. Not after everything he's done to us and Sofia."

General Johnson raised his hand. "Pretend to join forces with him. Take care of Mateo, then focus your attention on Mr. White."

Liam shook his head. "I don't trust him."

He stepped closer to the General. "And I don't trust you. Why are you here, given your repeated attempts to kill us and Sofia? What's in this for you?"

General Johnson placed a hand on Liam's shoulder. "A clear conscience, possibly at the end. I reflected on frequent past errors during the Hovercopter ride. My wife was on my mind. She'd be ashamed of who I've become since her murder."

He paused, his voice softening. "I used to care about doing right. After her death, my focus shifted to Mr. White's idea of the 'greater good'. I was so consumed by grief, and Mr. White helped me channel it. He delivered the people responsible for killing her on a platter. After that, I threw myself into the job. Only after you defeated me did I see it clear. I was fighting against what's ethical in this situation."

The General squeezed Liam's shoulder. "You and your friends were right, and I was wrong."

Liam stared into his eyes. "That was a gracious speech, touching, even. But if life's taught me anything, it's that actions speak louder than words."

He slithered from the General's grip and moved away.

Liam turned to James. "What's your opinion, buddy?"

James cupped his hands. "I agree with the General."

Liam spun around. "Anyone else want to plunge a knife into my back?"

James crossed his arms. "Do you have a better idea?"

Liam scratched his head. "Yeah, of course. I... uh, got a, er, strategy."

James shook his head. "No, you don't."

Liam looked at him and sighed. "No, I don't have a plan."

James pointed to General Johnson. "His approach makes sense."

He gestured at the forcefield. "Time isn't on our side. We can't search the entire city looking for him. So, unless anyone else has a better idea, I suggest we follow the General's lead."

James looked around at the group. Everyone nodded in agreement. Liam did so begrudgingly.

James turned back to General Johnson. "Okay, so what now?"

The General pointed to Lincoln Tower. "First, we need to get there. The Warehouse holds useful items for the upcoming fight against Mateo, the Taken, the Pallid, and Mr. White."

James nodded. He glanced around and noticed Robert wasn't standing with the group anymore. James spotted him near the edge of the roof, staring at the forcefield.

He walked over and stopped beside him. Robert's face glowed red from the light of the barrier.

James set a hand on Robert's shoulder. "I want you to realize how proud I am of you. You've handled everything we've been through better than most people would have. What happened to your mom was unfair, but we'll make it right."

He squeezed his son's arm and smiled at him. Robert turned to James, with a tear running down his face.

James wiped it away. "Is your mother on your mind?"

Robert shook his head. "No, Dad. I need to tell you something. It's been eating at me, and I need you to know."

James nodded. "Of course, buddy. You can share anything with me."

Robert sighed and gazed once more at the forcefield. "When it seemed like all of you were dead, I hated you."

James did a double take. "You hated me?"

Robert gave a nod. "I wondered why you would risk your life like you had nothing to live for. Like I didn't matter. Mateo took Mom from me, and I thought I'd lost you too. If all three of you died, I would have been alone. I sat there for hours, debating whether to end it all."

He held up his fingers, his voice trembling. "I was this close to doing it. But then I thought about her. She'd be furious with me for even having that idea. Then I remembered all the lessons you've taught me. To never quit, no matter how terrible things seem, to persevere through adversity. Thinking about you stopped me."

James pulled him into a tight hug, holding him close.

Then he held Robert by the shoulders, looking into his eyes. "I'm so sorry my actions caused you such distress. Have you experienced suicidal thoughts before?"

Robert shook his head. "No, I'm not suicidal. I've never been. But living alone in a world full of Taken..."

He paused, his voice steady yet heavy with emotion. "I didn't see any reason to be alive. With everything we'd seen until that moment, it felt like a battle we would lose without you three. And I refused to become a Reaper. That was my worst-case scenario. Worse than death. Serving her killer would have been unbearable. I'd rather die than be one of the Taken."

Robert turned to his father, his eyes glassy but resolute. "But in the end, I couldn't quit. I couldn't stop thinking about how much it would hurt you both if I did. I felt I would disappoint you and Mom if I didn't fight for every moment. Eventually, I'll come to terms with the fact that she's gone. I'm sad, and I will always miss her, but the thought of losing you too...it was almost overwhelming."

James nodded, his gaze unwavering. "I am so sorry you had to feel that way because of my actions. But I need you to know something. I didn't risk everything because I had nothing to live for."

He took a deep breath. "I had much to look forward to, so I drank the formula. You've always been my main reason, Robert. All my efforts have been to make sure you grow up and have a full life. And Sofia..."

James hesitated for a moment. "I hoped to see where things went with her. She gave me hope. But I also needed to stop Mateo, to make him pay for everything he's done to us.

Especially to you."

He shook his head, his expression grave. "Using that formula seemed like the best way to achieve our goals. If this is the end, I want to go down trying to protect everyone. Not just you and our friends, but the entire city."

James looked at the forcefield. "Evil wins when good men do nothing. After all I've tried to teach you, how hypocritical would I be if I stood by and let everything fall apart? I didn't know if Evolution would work, but I had to become the man I needed to be to get the job done."

Robert was quiet, staring at the forcefield as though searching for answers in its red glow. He turned back to James, his voice steady but firm. "You realize Mateo has to die, right?"

James shook his head, meeting his son's gaze. "He might be the only one who can fix this in time to save those trapped with the Taken and the Pallid. If he dies, that hope ends."

Robert's expression darkened. "And what makes you so sure he can stop this?"

James shrugged. "I'm not. We're hoping that while Mateo created the Taken, he also developed an antidote. In case things got out of hand. But after everything he discussed with Mr. White, I doubt he did. That doesn't mean he can't."

Robert grabbed his father's shoulder. "What makes you think he'll even try to make one?"

James remained silent.

Robert shook his head. "It's obvious to me what needs to be done. I don't see how it isn't clear to everyone else. Mateo caused all this chaos over the past two days. Everything we've been through is his fault. His death is justified, and it's necessary. He got away, and now we're all trapped under this forcefield."

James shook his head. "You don't know that. They built the barrier to contain the monsters."

Robert pointed toward the General. "Do you think you understand Mr. White better than he does?"

James sighed and shook his head again.

Robert gestured emphatically. "General Johnson didn't just say the forcefield stopped the Taken; he said The Agency put it up because they believe Mateo is still inside. Mr. White thinks he is the worst monster of them all. And Mr. White's willing to sacrifice everyone to stop him."

James stared at him. "Nothing is inevitable unless you stop seeking alternatives or give up. The biggest difference between me and Mr. White is that I believe nobody should be sacrificed, but he will let people die for his version of the greater good. No matter how bad it looks, this situation might still be salvageable. Death isn't the only solution."

Liam placed a hand on James' shoulder. "What if Robert is right?"

James turned and saw Liam and Jessica standing behind him. He studied their expressions. "How much did you hear?"

Jess reached out, caressing his face. "Most of it."

He caressed her fingers. "Do you agree with them?"

She shrugged. "I'm not sure yet. But I don't see why we can't try both approaches. We need to convince Mateo to undo what he's done. If he refuses, or if Mateo's too far gone, then we'll have no choice but to stop him before he causes even more damage."

James glanced at their faces before turning to Robert. "If Mateo needs to die, it won't be by your hand. Promise me you will not try to kill him."

Robert met his father's gaze and nodded. "I promise, Dad."

James gripped Robert's shoulder, offering him a reassuring smile.

He turned to Liam. "Take Robert and head to Lincoln Tower. I'll meet you there."

Liam searched James' eyes. "Are you okay?"

James gave a nod. "Yeah. I just need a moment."

He stepped onto the ledge, but Jess grabbed his hand. James faced her as she mounted beside him.

She smiled. "I'm going with you."

He looked at her. "Hold on tight."

She nodded, gripping her arms around his back.

With a powerful leap, they took off, soaring through the air as Liam and the others headed toward Lincoln Tower.

Chapter Five

James and Jessica soared above the red-tinged buildings of Downtown Allegheny, the frigid air whipping through her curly black hair. She clung to him, her hands pressed against his chest, her legs wrapped around his waist. Jess leaned in and kissed the back of his neck. "I know you're thinking about Robert."

He shook his head, exhaling. "It's a lot to process. To find out his mother was being abused by Lex, and neither of them told me."

James fell silent for a moment, his thoughts racing. '*Why didn't they tell me? Did they think I'd do nothing?*' he thought.

He continued. "I would've helped. Protected them from him."

James glanced over his shoulder at her. "Losing his mom, believing he also lost me...it's hardened him. And I hate that I played a part in that... in this coldness."

She rested her head against his back, hugging him tighter. "You did what you had to do to protect him. Taking the Evolution formula was a risk, but how else would you have stood up to Mr. White's agents, the Taken, and the Pallid? Without it, we would've died at the research campus. You made the right call. Because of you, we have a fighting chance...us and the entire city. You were selfless, James."

He shook his head. "Yeah, but at what cost? If I save Allegheny but lose my son to cold-heartedness, then I'm a hero who failed as a father."

Jess shook her head. "As long as Robert is alive, you haven't failed. The lessons don't end until you're gone, and that won't be anytime soon. Were you always a perfect child? Did you never have gloomy thoughts?"

James nodded.

She rubbed his chest with her thumb. "We all experience moments like that. Most of us resist our darker impulses. That's why most people are decent human beings. The world has seen dark times. Robert is going to be okay."

Jess smiled. "Do you know why I fell in love with you?"

He smirked. "My mesmerizing looks."

She chuckled. "Your physical appearance attracted me to you, but your strength captured me. The determination you have to never give up and keep pushing forward, no matter the situation or who doubted you. How you motivated me to be my best, how you always supported everything I wanted to do. Even if you didn't understand it at first, you would learn, just to help me chase my goals."

Jess tightened her grip on him with her right hand and legs.

She caressed James' face with her left hand. "I want you to know that I forgive you for beginning a new relationship."

He looked back at her.

Jess smiled. "You thought I was dead. You mourned me and went through so much unnecessary pain. I'm sorry you experienced that. All because those doctors wouldn't let me contact you. If they had, I would have stayed. I supported what they were trying to do after seeing all those people and my best friends die."

She cleared her throat. "I understand why Sofia interests you. She's a gorgeous woman. But after fighting so hard to return to you, I won't give you up now. When this situation is over, let's get married like we planned."

James smiled. "You being here is still unreal. I'm just savoring every moment. To hear your voice, feel your touch, and see your smile. With this forcefield trapping us, it's difficult to imagine the future. But that's definitely something we'll discuss. First, I have to focus on getting everyone through what comes next."

Jess shook her head. "Coming back to you motivated me. Thinking of marrying you. Becoming Robert's stepmom and having children together. I imagined raising a family with you, seeing the world, growing old by your side. Those thoughts kept me alive then, and they'll keep me going now. I've already waited a year to marry you. Once we make it through this, I refuse to wait another second. I don't care if it's just us and Robert, I want to finally be Mrs. Jessica Williams."

He slowed to a hover, shifting Jess from his back to his front. James gazed into her eyes and smiled. She leaned in, and they kissed. Their embrace tightened as the passion deepened.

He pulled away.

A puzzled look flashed across her face. "What's wrong?"

James held a finger to his lips, signaling for silence.

After a brief pause, he looked at her. "Hold on tight."

James shot toward Lincoln Tower at top speed, Jess secure in his arms.

She peered up at him as they flew. "What's happening?"

He looked straight ahead. "Another Hovercopter is on its way."

Chapter Six

The Hovercopter was silent except for the whir of the engine. Isaac was in the copilot's seat while Colonel Brian piloted. General Johnson sat in the middle side chair alone behind the Colonel, missing his cybernetic left arm. Liam held it in the opposite side seats, with Emily on his right behind Isaac. Robert rested alone in the back row.

Liam walked over and crouched beside Isaac and smirked.

Isaac stared at him. "What's so funny?"

Liam shook his head. "You wouldn't get it."

Isaac folded his arms. "Try me."

Liam shrugged. "Okay. I was just thinking that being able to run fast isn't such a bad superpower after all. Then I wondered at what speed I'd have to sprint against the Earth's rotation to reverse time. It's the only way to turn your dusty bones solid again."

Isaac shook his head. "I wish I didn't know you had powers."

Liam folded his arms. "Why not? With these abilities, I'm a super cop. I can do remarkable things."

Isaac turned towards him. "I don't doubt that, but there are consequences. What happens if you're focused on chasing a criminal, and a mother and her child step out in front of you? Have you mastered controlling your agility at this speed?"

Liam shook his head.

Isaac held out a hand. "What if you run straight through them? If criminals discover your secret, those near you become vulnerable. Everyone you care about would be in danger."

'*Here we go again.*' Liam thought.

He leaned back. "You always find a problem where it doesn't exist."

Isaac sighed. "I'm not trying to be negative. But knowing about your abilities makes me think of potential risks. Ones I fear you won't take seriously. That's what will keep me up at night and cost me my remaining gray hair. Which is why I'd rather not know. So I can live a normal life without worrying about you."

Liam placed a hand over his chest. "Are you saying you *haven't* worried about me being a cop?"

He shook his head. "So, the truth comes out."

Isaac sighed. "I believe you're missing my point."

Liam stood. "I'm not, but I don't want to talk about this anymore."

He started walking, but Isaac grabbed his wrist. "Promise me you'll always use your powers responsibly."

Liam nodded. "Of course I will. I'll play some, maybe ninety pranks, but being a cop comes first, superhero second."

He winked at Isaac, who chuckled. Then Liam moved seats and sat next to Emily. She was staring out the window at the crimson dome.

He tapped her knee. "While you were gone, I felt the same way as you did. I missed you and regretted not seeing you for what we might have been together."

Emily smiled at him. "You better have. Did you try to ignore the feelings like I did?"

He nodded. "I tried. When you disappeared, I was mad, but I didn't understand why. At first, I told myself I was just upset that you left, nothing more. But the more passed, the clearer it became. I had missed my chance."

She placed a hand on his face. "Time away opened my eyes to what I didn't acknowledge."

They exchanged smiles.

She cleared her throat. "Did you date anyone while I was gone? I bet you had to fight women off with a stick."

He shook his head. "If I did that, I'd have to arrest myself. Besides, I'm already married to the job. She'd get jealous if I brought someone else into our relationship."

Liam pointed at Emily. "You were the one breaking hearts in Silver City. Crying guys who were less handsome but wealthier than me probably litter the streets."

Emily chuckled. "When I wasn't working, I was feeling guilty. About how I left my dad, about not doing more to help him, about not telling you and Isaac what was happening. And I felt bad for ignoring you. Being away from you made me realize how much I wanted you."

He rubbed her knee. "What took you so long to return to Allegheny? And when you did, why didn't you tell me?"

She placed her hand over his. "I returned as soon as I thought it was necessary. But until I figured out how to help my father, I wasn't going to burden you and Isaac."

Liam shook his head. "We're experts at carrying burdens. It's part of the job. We would've helped because we love you both."

Emily nodded. "You're right. I should have spoken with you both, and I shouldn't have gone. So much could have been different."

Liam clasped her hand. "I wish we'd had this talk sooner, but I'm glad we're having it now. Once we get through this, we'll make sure your dad gets the help he needs."

She smiled. "And what about us?"

He smirked. "Was I not clear enough? I thought the 'we' in my last statement implied me and you. Dusty Bones can tag along if he wants."

Emily leaned in and kissed him, then pulled back, tracing his face with her fingers. "Will you be my boyfriend?"

Liam shook his head.

She crossed her arms. "Why not?"

He gestured toward the forcefield. "Once we defeat the bad guys and all their monsters, we'll be together."

Emily took his hands. "We already know we want to be a couple. Why wait any longer?"

Liam stared at her. "James and Sofia started dating yesterday after months of unspoken attraction. They stopped wasting time. I understood it, but I disagreed with it. That's their choice, and this is mine."

He squeezed her hand. "We'll be with each other soon. But right now, I need to concentrate on what matters, so I can focus on who is important."

She nodded. "I get it. I don't agree, but I'll wait."

Liam kissed her cheek. "Good. Because James's ex-fiancée just showed up out of nowhere, and I have to make sure your secret former fiancé doesn't pop up."

Emily punched him in the shoulder. He rubbed his arm. "Rule number one, refrain from bruising the superhero."

Liam and Emily chuckled. Then he held up his hand, his expression turning serious.

She frowned. "What is it?"

He focused his hearing and scanned the reflections in the surrounding buildings with his eyes. Then he swung toward the front. "There's another Hovercopter on us!"

Isaac checked the cameras, spotting their pursuer. He turned to Brian. "Lose that 'copter!"

Colonel Brian banked hard to the right, weaving around a building, but the other aircraft followed. He flew over a rooftop, then through an open archway built into a high-rise, but their tail stayed locked on them.

Liam shook his head. "It's still on us."

The other Hovercopter pulled up beside them.

A familiar voice crackled over the speaker. "Land, and let's talk."

Liam groaned, rubbing his face in frustration. "I am so tired of Mr. Shite."

He stuck up his middle finger at the side window.

Mr. White's tone remained calm. "Liam, that isn't behavior befitting a police captain. Please tell Brian and your father to set down the aircraft."

Liam shook his head and kept his middle finger raised.

A blue blur shot toward them from the front.

James flew alongside, then placed Jess inside their Hovercopter. "Get to Lincoln Tower. I'll handle this."

He dropped back to hover behind them as they continued across the river. A blue aura engulfed his body.

The pursuing aircraft came to a halt.

James shifted to its left side and gripped the handle. Before he could force it, the door slid open on its own. He entered and proceeded to the pilot's seat, only to find a reinforced door separating it from the cabin.

James opened it.

There sat a hologram of Mr. White, puffing on a cigar.

Mr. White smirked. "Were you expecting to see me in here?"

James powered down. "I figured you'd stay far away from a group of people you've tried to kill multiple times."

Mr. White exhaled a slow puff of smoke. "I've only attempted to eliminate you once, when I found out you stole what was mine. Any other attempt you speak of was the General's doing."

James held up his hand. "That's still twice by Agency personnel. What do you want?"

Mr. White took another drag of his cigar. "Something big is coming. I'm offering you a second chance to be on the right side."

James crossed his arms. "From where I stand, the ones opposing us are Mateo, the Taken, the Pallid, and you. So, I'd say we're already on the right side."

Mr. White shook his head. "I opposed you in a moment of anger over your transgression. Just days ago, I welcomed you to my agency and accepted your help on a mission. Even after your betrayal, I was willing to forgive you all, and you refused my offer earlier, as you're doing now."

He took another slow puff. "I've seen how fiercely devoted you are to Robert and your companions. Let me assure you, joining me is the only way to survive what's coming. The only means of keeping them safe. If you refuse, you are all doomed."

James shook his head. "Even if everything you claim is true, I'll have to pass. Trying to kill me is one thing, but my son? My fiancée? My friends? That's another. You can't mess with the people I love and think we can ever be cool."

His gaze hardened. "We'll see you soon, but it won't be to join you. It'll be to stop you."

Mr. White stared at him. "Please take your time before deciding. Refusing my offer will endanger most, if not all of you."

James crossed his arms. "What's coming?"

Mr. White shook his head. "You'll only find out if you ally with me."

James let out a short laugh. "I doubt Liam would ever work with you. And I suspect you don't even want him to."

Mr. White took a slow puff of his cigar. "Are you willing to put Liam before Robert and Jessica?"

James said nothing; his expression was unreadable.

Mr. White extinguished his cigar. "Consider your decision, but do it fast. Make the choice that's best for you and your family. Time is running out."

James turned and exited the aircraft. It veered away, heading back toward The Agency.

He flew straight to the helipad on Lincoln Tower, where Colonel Brian had landed.

Brian, Isaac, General Johnson, Liam, Emily, Robert, and Jessica stood in a circle.

As James touched down in front of them, Liam stepped forward. "What did Mr. Shite want?"

James looked at each of them, his gaze lingering on Jess and Robert. "Mr. White said something big is coming. He wants us to join him. Mr. White claims time is running out, and if we don't, we're all doomed."

Chapter Seven

Sofia and Andrea floated down to The Warehouse via the GravLift. The artificial gravity's heavy pressure kept them from free-falling.

Andrea turned to Sofia. "Whose code did you use to access the lift?"

Sofia glanced at her mother. "I saw both Colonel Brian's and General Johnson's codes. I used Brian's."

Andrea smiled. "Way to be attentive."

Sofia grinned in response. "Just like you taught me."

They exited the GravLift and walked toward The Warehouse. At the entrance, they moved to input passcodes on opposite panels. With a click, the door unlocked, and they stepped inside.

Sofia looked over at Andrea. "Earlier, General Johnson peered into a crate, and whatever he saw shook him. I want to know what's in the box."

Andrea nodded and followed as Sofia led the way. They hurried through the aisles of boxes, each containing secrets of The Agency, until they reached the crates.

Sofia turned to Andrea. "You're familiar with Mr. White. Should I find out what's inside the box?"

Andrea shook her head. "If whatever's in that crate made Oliver nervous, probably not."

Sofia took a deep breath and stepped closer. She placed her hands on the top, then glanced at her mother. An aura flared around Andrea's fists. Sofia pulled her right hand away and powered it up too.

With her left hand, she removed the lid and leaned back. When nothing jumped out, she moved closer to examine the contents.

She slapped her left palm over her mouth. "Oh my God."

Andrea rushed to her side. "What is it?"

She stared into the crate, frozen for a moment. "How?"

Sofia turned to Andrea. "Did Mr. White try to make his own Taken?"

Andrea nodded. "Seems like he at least tried."

'Why would he attempt to create his own version of Taken?' Sofia wondered.

She leaned over the box again. "Well, he skipped a few steps. It looks... weird. The Taken's way smaller, all mouth and teeth, the claws are longer, and the thighs are huge. That's more unsettling than any Taken I've seen."

Andrea chuckled.

Sofia turned to her. "What's so funny?"

Andrea gave her a knowing glance. "Your father once told me that while he worked in the lab Mr. White provided, he never trusted his intentions. Years ago, he created a system to encode his research. You need a specific passkey to decode each formula."

She pointed into the crate. "Someone's replication effort, lacking the key, yielded this."

Sofia shook her head. "If this is an Agency scientist's attempt, when would they have done it? Could they try to figure out his encoding system?"

Andrea turned to Sofia. "Let's hope not. If they do, Lord only knows what could happen."

Sofia slammed her fist against the crate. "General Johnson knew about this two days ago and didn't say a word. He let our group keep going with the mission to stop the Taken, while the guy who sent us was busy trying to make his own. How could he carry on like this doesn't change everything?"

Andrea placed a hand on Sofia's shoulder. "Perhaps he chose the operation as the top priority. Maybe he thought this situation was secondary."

Sofia shook her head. "Or maybe he's just loyal to The Agency."

Andrea gave her shoulder a gentle squeeze. "He used to be different, but I guess time will tell. Come on, let's keep moving."

They crossed to the opposite end of The Warehouse and exited into The Web. Three hallways stretched ahead. One to the northeast, a path to the northwest, and a route leading straight north.

They took the northern hallway, which they'd traveled separately before, following it to its terminus.

At the top of the steps, Sofia entered General Johnson's code, and they stepped into his office.

Andrea turned to Sofia. "Look for something useful. Anything we can use against Mr. White."

Sofia nodded.

Andrea examined the bookshelf while Sofia searched through the desk.

The upper drawers held normal items.

Papers, fancy pens, and monogrammed envelopes.

Then she opened the bottom right drawer and paused. Reaching in, she pulled out a photograph.

Sofia turned to her mother with the picture in her hand. "What the hell is this?"

Andrea walked over, glanced at the photo, and fell silent.

Sofia pointed at it. "Why are you and General Johnson holding hands?"

Andrea took the image from Sofia's grasp and studied it for a moment. "A local photographer shot this at dinner. This was before you were born."

She sighed. "Your father and I were working on a joint research project for our government in Thailand. It was a year-long assignment. Within the first week, thieves broke in and stole equipment from our facility. The administration sent replacements and military protection. That's when we met Oliver."

Andrea looked at Sofia. "Mateo is a very resolute man. During that project, he focused on his work and ignored me. Even after hours, he'd ignore me and spend his nights buried in his notes. I mentioned my feelings of neglect over the months. But nothing changed. So eventually, I stopped trying. I felt alone."

She looked back down at the photo. "One night, I was having dinner by myself, again, when Oliver came over to my table. He told me I was too pretty to look that sad. I smiled. Oliver returned the smile and asked to sit. That evening, he did something your father hadn't done in months. He saw me, and he listened. I felt valued by Oliver, a feeling that had been absent for some time."

Andrea sat on the edge of the desk. "Dinner with him became a regular event. I was tired of eating alone, and he was a great friend. Your dad noticed I'd stopped asking for his time. That's when he realized he might lose me. Mateo started showing me the type of interest I missed from before our trip. So, I went to tell Oliver I couldn't dine with him anymore. Now that Mateo was paying attention again, he'd notice. At that moment, Oliver confessed his feelings to me. And I had affections for him too. More than I should have. One thing led to another... and I slept with him."

Sofia gasped. "You cheated on Papa?"

Andrea sighed. "After I realized my mistake, I left. I avoided Oliver, even when he tried to talk to me. Soon after, I discovered my pregnancy."

Sofia covered her mouth in shock.

Andrea placed a hand on her daughter's shoulder. "I convinced Mateo to leave the project because I was pregnant. He was eager to become a father.

I was relieved to distance myself from Oliver, to get away from my mistake. I had a friend run a D.N.A. test to confirm if you were Mateo's."

She looked at her.

Sofia's expression shifted.

Concern colored her voice. "What is it?"

Andrea squeezed her hand. "The results confirmed you are Mateo's. I was so happy. So relieved. I don't know what I would have done if he hadn't been your father."

She shook her head. "I wouldn't have lied to him. After everything we'd been through, I would've owed him the truth. Even then, despite the distance between us, I couldn't imagine happiness without him in my life. Not then. Not now."

She let out a soft laugh. "I'd be lying if I said I never wondered what might've happened if Mateo hadn't come to his senses. If I had pursued Oliver... how different would my story be?"

Sofia reached for her mother's hand. "Do you regret staying with Papa?"

Andrea beamed. "Not for one second. Once you were born, he was laser-focused on our family. His goal was to be a better husband and the best father he could be. I became a priority again. The man I fell in love with returned to me."

She rubbed Sofia's fingers. "Besides, I understand it's impossible to determine what might have happened with Oliver. So why agonize over the choice? I believed I had made the right one, and I was mostly correct. Never knowing the future I might've had with him is fine. Maybe if I had chosen him, I'd have died on vacation. Life is unpredictable. I followed my gut, and it led me to where I wanted to be, with Mateo. Following my heart brought me you."

Sofia smiled. "Thanks Mama."

Andrea kissed her daughter's forehead. "You're welcome, *mi Princesa.* We should get moving."

They stood and approached the faux wall. Andrea sighed.

Sofia turned to her. "What is it?"

Andrea shook her head as the steel gate lifted. "Leaving your father then might have prevented this. He wouldn't have tried to save me or needed to avenge what happened."

As the partition rose, Sofia looked at her mother. "If you had known all this then, would it have changed your decision?"

Andrea peered through the forcefield into the empty office. "Possibly. I never wanted to hurt innocent people."

She summoned an energy bubble around them and disabled the barrier. The shielding displaced the floating Remnant in the front office. Leaving the building, they surveyed the street and rooftops. Once they were sure they were alone, they made their way toward Lemon Station.

They moved past the red-tinged buildings, walking down the pitch-black road. When they arrived at the terminal, they exchanged a nod, preparing to enter. Sofia formed her own energy bubble, and both women powered up their hands. They stepped inside, ready to face whatever danger awaited them, but only darkness greeted them.

Sofia moved toward the tracks. "The train's gone. We'll have to find another way."

They floated down onto the railway and raced through the tunnel, gliding just above the rails. White and yellow energy trails streamed behind them as they sped down hills and around bends. As they neared the station beneath The Agency, Andrea slowed and signaled for Sofia to stop. Both landed silently.

Andrea crept forward with Sofia in tow. They halted at the edge of the train platform.

Red emergency lights flashed at slow intervals, each burst of light revealing an area teeming with dozens of Pallid.

Between flashes, darkness swallowed everything.

Sofia turned to Andrea. "What now? Should we return to the nearest station and enter through The Agency's main entrance?"

Andrea shook her head. "No. There's no time to waste. We must save your father from himself and stop this madness."

She pivoted to face the swarm of Pallid. "We'll fight through them."

Sofia stared at her. "That's insane. We have to stay alive if we're going to protect Papa and end this. Fighting that many won't be a cakewalk."

Andrea gave her daughter a small smile. Her energy bubble condensed into a suit of glowing body armor, then in a flash, she shot forward.

Sofia reached out. "Mama!"

Without hesitation, she formed her own energy armor and chased after her mother.

Andrea stopped behind the HoverTrain.

She raised her hands, psychokinetically detaching one car from the rest. It floated for a moment, then Andrea tossed it upward.

The car crashed sideways into the middle of the horde, crushing half the Pallid and cracking the concrete.

The remaining twenty Pallid turned toward Andrea, baring their teeth.

Sofia leaped into the air on the platform's right side. The creatures shifted their attention to her just before she slammed into them, fists first, and landed hard on the left end of the platform.

Andrea charged forward, flinging Pallid upwards one after another. With sharp flicks of her wrist, she hurled them into the surrounding rock wall near the elevator. Andrea intercepted those who pounced at her midair, crushing them with a flash of kinetic force.

Sofia weaved through attacks, blasting the last of the Pallid with focused bursts of energy. The platform fell silent.

Andrea caught her breath and smiled at Sofia. "See? We took care of them."

Sofia shook her head. "That could've gone a lot differently. You're exhausted. We should've had a strategy before attacking."

Andrea straightened. "We don't have time to strategize."

From the left tunnel, a chorus of guttural roars echoed. They both snapped their attention in that direction and saw hundreds of Pallid pouring out.

Sofia groaned. "Now we have no chance to plan."

She dashed to the elevator and input General Johnson's passcode. The panel flashed red. Sofia tried Colonel Brian's code with the same result.

She turned to her mother. "The codes aren't working!"

They exchanged a look, then faced the oncoming horde, readying for battle. The Pallid closed in fast.

A ding sounded behind them.

They rushed into the elevator. Just as the doors began to close, a handful of Pallid wedged themselves into the gap, forcing it open, clawing to reach them. Andrea and Sofia struck the ones blocking the doorway, but more piled in the rear, making it impossible to push them back.

Andrea dropped to her knees and pressed her hands to the floor. Energy rippled from her palms onto the ground, surging past the threshold. With a sharp upward motion, she flung the creatures standing on the energy path high into the air. The pallid flew in every direction, slamming against the platform as the doors slid shut.

They retreated to the back wall of the elevator, breathing hard.

Sofia glanced at her mother, concern in her eyes.

Andrea met her gaze. "What?"

Before Sofia could respond, a flicker of light appeared in front of them. Mr. White's smirking hologram materialized. "That was impressive."

Andrea crossed her arms. "I'm not here to impress you."

His smile widened. "I know why you're here, and I've been expecting you."

Chapter Eight

The freezing wind stung their faces and hands as they stood on the rooftop, discussing Mr. White's proposal. Emily crossed her arms. "We should at least consider it."

General Johnson looked at her. "You shouldn't entertain the idea. My plan is the better one. Through my mistakes, I've learned we can't trust him."

Liam chuckled. "So, we're supposed to ignore him and rely on you instead? That reeks of hypocrisy."

The General held up his hand. "I understand why you don't believe me. I haven't earned your confidence. But I'm not asking for it. I urge you to use your instincts. If your gut tells you to join him, then go ahead."

Emily stepped closer to General Johnson. "Feeling uneasy isn't enough to dismiss intuition. Yes, I have doubts, but I still think this might be the smarter move compared to fighting him again."

James moved forward. "General Johnson is right. Trusting Mr. White would be a mistake. He ordered agents to kill us less than an hour ago."

James pointed at Liam. "He wants what we carry inside of us. How far will he go to get it?"

James shook his head. "I'm not risking my life, or the lives of Robert and Jess, by siding with him."

He paused. "Let's vote on it. Who thinks we should join him?"

James scanned their faces and stopped when he saw Emily's raised hand. "You think we should team up with him?"

Emily lowered her hand. "We should at least hear him out."

She looked around. "I just want everybody to be safe. If joining is the way to do that, we should listen. He knows what's coming; we don't."

James walked over and placed a hand on her shoulder. "Protecting everyone is why we shouldn't accept his offer. But we'll give him a chance to speak. If we dislike what we hear, we stop him. Hopefully, Mateo's already on his way and we can deal with both of them."

He turned around. "Isaac and Brian, take Emily and General Johnson to The Agency in the Hovercopter and wait for us there. We're right behind you. I want to check Jack Lincoln's office to see if there's anything useful."

James turned to the General. "I'm trusting my gut."

General Johnson smiled. "About the items I mentioned earlier, stop at The Warehouse. In section eleven, find box twenty-five. Within section three, locate container twenty-two. You'll discover tools there to help in the fight at The Agency."

James nodded. "Thank you, General."

Liam gave the General a sideways glance. "Are you trying to trick me? Is Medusa's head in one of those boxes? Gonna turn everyone to stone and leave us frozen for eternity?"

General Johnson raised a hand. "No tricks. I promise."

The General took a deep breath. "After what I've experienced the last couple of days, I'm thinking about everything I did over the past few years."

General Johnson patted his chest. "One good deed isn't enough. Hell, a hundred might

not be enough for my actions, but it's a start."

He chuckled. "Besides, you're so fast, you'd run off before anything happened."

Liam stroked his chin. "You right, you right."

The General and Colonel Brian handed James and Liam the codes they'd need to access Lincoln Tower and The Warehouse.

James extended his hand. "Thank you, General."

General Johnson smiled and shook it. "Don't thank me yet. We still have a fight ahead. Be grateful when we've won."

James nodded, and the General turned to board the Hovercopter. Colonel Brian's departure with others found Jess and Robert leading the descent of the emergency stairwell, engrossed in discussion. James and Liam followed a few steps behind them.

Liam leaned over. "How are you doing?"

James looked at him. "As good as I can be, considering everything that's happened."

Liam raised an eyebrow. "You're okay with the whole situation?"

James nodded. "I've accepted Sofia's decision to leave. I just wish she'd told me where she was going before she left."

Liam smiled. "I hate when they do that."

James returned the smile. "I'm just glad Jess is alive. Her memorial was the hardest thing I have ever experienced, and I refuse to go through that hell again. I'll do whatever it takes to protect her. Losing her a second time isn't an option."

They watched Robert laugh at something Jess said.

James smiled. "If something happened to me, she would care for him as if he were her own, because she sees him that way. She treats him as if he were her son."

Liam clapped James on the back. "Love and loyalty like that is rare. The thought of reaching you kept her going for a year. You're lucky to have a second chance, if you choose to accept it. Few find devotion such as Jess'."

James turned to Liam. "How would you handle this situation? My heart and head agree, but my gut's still holding out."

Liam shook his head. "I plead the Fifth on your love life. But I will say this, listen to your heart, your brain, and your instincts. Consider each choice and choose wisely. Not future you. Not past you. The present you. What's done is done, and tomorrow might not play out how you imagine."

James threw an arm around Liam, and they both smiled as they entered Jack Lincoln's office.

Jess turned and grinned at the sight of them. "Why are you two grinning?"

Liam held up a hand. "That information is classified."

Jess smirked at James. "I believe I can get it out of him later."

James gave her a smile.

Liam glanced between them. "And on that note, I'll begin searching this place. My mind will be there. Our minds should ALL be there."

Jess walked over to James and rubbed his back. "Let's start over there."

He went behind the broken desk. "I'm going to check the drawers. Let me know if you see anything."

Jess nodded and began scanning the room. She viewed Liam and Robert searching the area near the GravLift. Turning, Jess noticed a lopsided portrait behind the desk. As she approached, Jess saw a sliver of exposed metal in the bottom right corner. She removed the painting and uncovered a hidden safe.

Jess tapped James on the shoulder. "Look at this."

He stood and turned around.

James examined the safe and observed the absence of a locking mechanism. "Liam, have you ever seen a safe like this?"

Liam turned and chuckled. "Have I? That's the Sparrow 2003. Best safe in the world. No dials, no keypads. This connects to the owner's

BrainLink. You could fire a cannon at it and not leave a dent. Whatever's inside stays there. Sorry, James."

Liam slapped the safe door, and it creaked open. "Unless some idiot left it unlocked."

He wrenched the door open and pulled out a stack of files.

Liam opened one and flipped through the pages. "This one's full of access codes and passwords."

James grabbed two other folders. "These are labeled Articles of Incorporation and Will, but they're both empty."

Jess looked at James. "Who would want these papers?"

He shook his head. "The question is, why take them?"

Liam glanced around. "We will not find the answer standing here. We've gotten everything we can from this place."

James nodded and headed toward the GravLift. "Whatever the General's sending us to retrieve had better be more useful than what we found here."

Liam stepped into the GravLift, followed by James, Robert, and Jess. They descended together. Once they exited, they moved to the double security doors.

James and Liam input the access codes General Johnson and Colonel Brian had given them.

The doors opened, and they made their way through The Warehouse until they reached section eleven.

They scanned the shelves until they spotted box twenty-five, the only metal container among the wooden ones. James and Liam dragged it out from the bottom shelf and entered the code to unlock it. After removing the lid, James handed Liam a sheet of paper and pulled out a black bodysuit that shimmered with hints of purple. Extra material was folded beside it.

Liam tapped the paper. "This is the Echo Bodysuit. According to the specs, the material is NanoKevlar and leather, reinforced with tungsten carbide lacing. It has energy receptors that charge when struck, and it's bulletproof. The smart fabric underlayer adapts to the wearer. The extra material can be used for other purposes."

Robert's eyes widened. "That's so cool. I want it."

James chuckled. "I bet you do. But are you sure? You haven't even seen what's in the other crate yet."

Robert smiled. "True enough."

He rubbed his hands together. "Let's go find out."

They located section three and found container twenty-two on the third shelf.

James flew up, retrieved the metal box, and placed it on the ground. After unlocking it and removing the lid, he handed Liam a sheet of paper and pulled out a helmet with a pouch attached to the bottom. The headgear was sleek and black, with square green glass eye slots.

Liam grinned at Robert. "You're going to want this one. It's called the Warlock Armor."

Robert examined it. "What does it do?"

Liam's grin widened. "Put on the helmet and think of the word 'armor.'"

James handed the headgear to Robert, who slipped it on and closed his eyes. The pouch burst open, and thousands of tiny black objects crawled out, skittering across his body until they interlocked like puzzle pieces. When they settled, he opened his eyes and looked down at himself. The suit now resembled carbon fiber, its surface formed by the miniature robots' interlocking legs. A green "W" glowed on the chest.

Robert beamed at his dad. "They're Microbots!"

James chuckled. "I know you're excited."

Liam nodded at Robert. "It's a Microbot suit. It could become whatever you imagine. Try thinking 'cape.'"

Robert shut his eyelids again. Microbots shifted from his sides and back, forming a short green cape.

He opened his eyes and turned to Liam. "What else can these do?"

Liam pointed at the paper. "First off, it doesn't say you need to close your eyes. The helmet reads your thoughts, so maybe stop doing that. It's kinda weird. Anyway, the Microbots can form weapons, bubbles, shields, anything you can picture. Oh, and you can fly too."

Robert hugged Jess, then looked her in the eyes. "This suit is mine. You'll have to pry it off my body if you want it."

She smiled and raised her hands in mock surrender. "It's all yours Robby."

He admired his new suit and hovered off the ground. Robert glanced at Liam. "How do I control this thing?"

Liam tapped his temple. "Your mind controls it. Just think about your destination and speed."

Robert extended his arms in front of him and rose into the air. He leveled out and drifted forward.

James handed the Echo Bodysuit to Jess, and they walked to another aisle. As Robert zipped around The Warehouse, practicing with his gear, she changed into hers. James kept watch, alert for any signs of Taken or Pallid nearby.

Jess tapped him on the shoulder. "So, how do I look?"

He turned to glance at her.

She posed in black boots that rose to mid-shin. The black NanoKevlar Leather suit clung to her frame, contoured by the smart fabric underlayer. Thin strands of purple tungsten carbide lacing ran up from her footwear along the sides of her legs, crisscrossed her waist and stomach, framed the curved V-neck, and extended over her shoulder blades down to her gloves. The bodysuit hugged her hips and thighs, with extra material draped from her shoulders to the small of her back like a cape. A few curls fell onto her face as she smiled at him.

James grinned. "Amazing. That suit fits you perfectly."

Jess returned the smile. "Thanks Jamie."

Robert landed beside them just as Liam appeared around the far corner. He looked at Liam. "The General came through with these suits."

Liam crossed his arms. "So he did. I still don't trust him."

James placed a hand on Liam's shoulder. "Trust him or not, he gave us two pieces of tech that will protect them and help win the fight."

He turned and started walking toward The Web. "Come on, let's head to General Johnson's office. After that, we go to The Agency."

Chapter Nine

Ice cubes clinked as Mr. White dropped them into his glass of bourbon. He swirled them while perched on the front of his black mahogany desk in his dimly lit office.

Mr. White took a sip and looked at Madam President Mary Jackson's hologram. "I knew what was coming. After the failed attempt to eliminate Mateo, I sent in a cleanup crew once he killed those agents. While sweeping The Warehouse, they reported several open boxes. When I discovered one of them contained E.M.P. bombs, I called in our infrastructure and tech teams to ensure our preparedness."

He chuckled. "We finished just before the explosions. Had we failed, Plan Delta would've been a no-go."

The President raised her wineglass toward him. "Thank goodness we still have a chance."

Mr. White took another sip. "Sometimes you're lucky; other times you're not. With the E.M.P.s, luck was on our side. With the Pallid, that wasn't the case. I heard the roar in the tunnels on Christmas Eve while I was communicating with General Johnson and the others. That sound was unfamiliar. It wasn't a Taken. Their mission was too critical to jeopardize, so I sent a second team to investigate."

She put her wineglass on the desk. "How did the investigation go?"

He took another sip. "When the agents arrived, they saw the creatures. Just as we were about to get a good look, communication was lost.

More agents investigated; but all traces of the creatures and personnel disappeared."

Mr. White stood, circled his desk, and lowered himself into his chair. "It's funny, isn't it?"

President Jackson looked at him. "What's funny?"

He smiled at her. "That feeling you get in your gut. The one that tells you something's wrong. No matter how prepared you are, unforeseen challenges can arise."

Mr. White took another sip. "I hadn't realized that feeling would lead to the Pallid. Although I have reservations about Plan Charlie, I don't see any other options."

He stared into his glass. "The unexpected can derail even the most carefully crafted plans. The Pallid are a major unforeseen variable."

She nodded. "True, but that was the reason we created the Allegheny Research Campus. To bring the brightest minds together. That's why we funded Mateo before he was aware of it. Why we backed Jack Lincoln on the strategic side. We aimed all our actions at protecting the continent's future in case of a significant threat. These weren't the threats we envisioned, but thankfully the infrastructure was in place."

President Jackson pointed at him. "Delegating top scientists to Plans Charlie and Delta for two years was fortuitous."

She shook her head. "If we hadn't established the campus then, what do you think would have happened? That team developed the forcefield containing both threats. Without it, it would only be a matter of time before both continents were overrun. Either killed or turned into Taken or Pallid."

Mr. White took another sip. "After the latest attempt on your life, I had to protect you from future attacks. The main reason I wanted the Evolution formula was for you."

He shared a faint smile. "Once ingested, it makes a person difficult to kill. Second, I desired it for myself. I already think I'm untouchable, but the formula would make that a certainty."

Mr. White swirled his drink around his cup. "The third motive was to create enhanced agents. That's why I needed both the vials and the formula."

He set his glass down. "When the exchange went sideways, I didn't panic. The equation was backed up on our servers. I had our science department reconstruct it. Once they completed it, I took it, but something was wrong. The Evolution formula shouldn't produce side effects, but I felt them right away. Skull-splitting headaches were the worst. When the scientists and I reviewed the process, we examined each step from beginning to end. Nothing appeared off until we realized the calculations might have been altered. We believe Mateo tampered with it."

President Jackson shook her head. "How is that even possible?"

Mr. White sighed. "Mateo is as brilliant as he is dangerous. If anyone could outmaneuver me, it's him."

He locked eyes with her. "There's something else. Since I took the corrupted version of the formula... it has been slowly killing me."

She stared at him. "Why am I only hearing this now?"

Mr. White gave a faint smile. "Because I knew you wouldn't accept that my plan to protect you is also my undoing. What good would telling you sooner have done?"

President Jackson leaned over her desk. "I would've assembled a team. The best doctors and scientists..."

He held up a hand. "Were already here. I had to evacuate them to a safer location. They told me there's nothing they can do without the original formula."

She studied his face. "You always have a solution for every situation. Tell me you have one now, to save your life."

Mr. White nodded. "I have a plan."

He picked up his drink and took another sip.

President Jackson crossed her arms. "But you will not inform me."

Mr. White shook his head. "No, I won't. Whether my plan succeeds or fails is irrelevant to what you need to do in the next phase of Plan Charlie. My role is mine, and yours is yours. Promise me you won't worry about me. I will be fine."

He smiled. "I always win in the end. Besides, you'll have more than enough on your plate without wondering if I succeeded."

She sighed. "At least tell me you're prepared if Mateo shows up."

Mr. White raised a finger. "When he shows up. He'll be here soon, and I'll be ready. I still have a couple of surprises for him. He sabotaged the Evolution formula, but other opportunities have presented themselves."

He smirked. "Mateo won't stop Plan Delta. Nothing will."

President Jackson sat on the edge of her desk. "What about the thieves?"

Mr. White raised another finger. "They will have one last chance to join me."

She held up three fingers. "And if they refuse you a third time?"

He chuckled. "I'll get them on my side. As always, I've put myself in a win-win situation. They don't realize it yet, but I have already won. All roads lead to The Agency, and by night's end, I will have most, if not all, of what I want. Plan Delta should proceed without a hitch."

President Jackson leaned forward. "I'm not sure that involving them is a good idea. We planned contingencies that didn't include them. They're wildcards, and they could derail everything."

Mr. White smiled. "You have assigned me significant responsibilities in the past. Are you doubting me now?"

She shook her head. "Of course not. I trust you. Your performance has been consistently excellent; however, this task holds significant weight. This is bigger than anything we've ever faced."

President Jackson crossed her arms. "I don't trust them. They might ruin Plan Delta."

He stood and leaned over the desk, pressing his finger twice on the top. "They may be the key to ensuring its success. Just...trust me. One more time."

She sighed. "Okay. I will, but...what if I can't do it?"

President Jackson shook her head. "What if I cannot bring myself to tell the people of this country what you've asked me to say?"

Mr. White stared at her. "Then something far worse shall be yours to tell them...the truth. And the questions that follow are going to be even harder to answer. My request presents difficulty; however, this method simplifies matters. Honesty would rob you of the chance to make things right."

She nodded. "It is easier, but is it the correct choice? What if it's the wrong one? How can we be sure there are no better options?"

He took a sip of bourbon. "Time has left us with two choices. Not three, not ten, not a hundred. Just two. And both suck. There is no best option, only the one that saves more lives. Wasting more energy debating what's 'right' would be another mistake. What matters now is understanding the worst-case scenarios and recognizing that our decision is necessary to prevent them. It will be tough, but you must persevere. And when the moment comes, I am confident you'll follow through."

President Jackson looked away. "How do you recover from this? Knowing that no matter what decisions you make, you still lose? Whether publicly or privately, you lose either way."

Mr. White finished his bourbon. "By remembering that these are thankless jobs. You keep going because, even when people are angry with you, you understand you did everything possible to protect them. We save them from threats they'll never know existed. You protected their freedom, so they still may criticize you."

He smiled. "Some careers earn people's love. In ours, half will hate you just because you're not their pick. Those who voted for you may also disagree with your decisions. But it remains our job to protect everyone on these continents. From themselves and from dangers they can't imagine. The anger is temporary. Prioritize the mission and allow external opinions to resolve themselves."

Mr. White checked his HoloWatch alert: "Andrea and Sofia are trying to access the tunnel elevator, and they're not alone."

He zoomed in on the fingerprint scanner and pressed his thumb to the watch. They rushed into the elevator as the doors opened.

Mr. White stood tall and straightened his tie. "Well, my oldest and dearest friend, this is goodbye, until we meet again."

She smiled. "I'll be waiting for you when you finish."

He returned the smile. "Then I'd better not disappoint you. I will see you soon. Right now, it's time to save the world."

Chapter Ten

General Johnson stared out the window of the Hovercopter. The red glow of the dome bathed the buildings below, while the bloodshed caused by the Taken and the Pallid stained the streets. He turned to Isaac. "Do you remember I told you about Senator Pennell? The one who blocked funding for the preventative measures?"

Isaac faced him. "Yeah, I remember."

The General sighed. "The reason he funded me was his son's kidnapping. He reached out to an agency friend of his. That acquaintance suggested he contact me to find his son. When I arrived at his office, his wife was inconsolable. He told me I could have whatever I needed for my project if I helped locate his child. I looked at his weeping spouse and agreed."

He turned to Isaac again. "That was one of the worst things I've ever done."

Isaac watched him. "What do you mean? Why was it so terrible?"

General Johnson lowered his head. "I saw that woman put all her hope in me...when I kidnapped her son."

Isaac scratched his head. "You did what?!"

The General stared at him. "I took him."

He paused. "My plan was to make it look like terrorists had taken him. The same extremists I had already defeated. The same ones I knew better than anyone. So, they would assign me to the mission to save him. I also had designs, which he had rejected out of spite, that would become useful in finding his son."

Isaac looked at him. "Wouldn't he recognize your face or your voice once you showed up as the savior?"

General Johnson shook his head. "He didn't see me before I knocked him unconscious. I blindfolded him, wore a mask, and used a vocal modifier. There's no way he could identify me."He looked back out the window. "Senator Pennell pulled strings to fast-track the funding. His contact brought in a manufacturer to bring my designs to life."

The General smirked for a second. "Within days, we had surveillance drones in the air, equipped with three-dimensional hologram recording. I coordinated their movements."

He turned to Isaac. "The plan was working. I was watching my vision materialize. By day, I oversaw manufacturing and planned my new anti-terrorist task force. By night, I relieved the lead agent on the search for Pennell's son. We looked everywhere except the one place he was."

General Johnson paused. "The evening before I intended to 'find' him, I discovered him dead in the location I was holding him."

Isaac shifted in his seat. "How did he die?"

The General shook his head. "That's what still haunts me. I spoke with him that morning. He begged me to let him go again. I told him I would. Initially he didn't believe me, but once I explained that hurting him was never part of the plan, he calmed. He seemed hopeful when I left."

General Johnson exhaled. "When I returned, he remained tied to the chair, but lifeless. I don't know how he died."

He paused. "I never meant for it to end that way."

Isaac crossed his arms. "How did you imagine it would turn out? You kidnapped Senator Pennell's son. Someone was going to get hurt, either him or you. Did you really think you'd covered your tracks and would just avoid consequences?"

The General turned to him. "I thought I had. But somebody knew where he was and who was holding him. Instead of freeing him, they killed him."

His fists tightened. "I kept asking myself why? Who would want him dead? Aside from being Senator Pennell's son, he was an ordinary civilian."

He turned towards Isaac and leaned forward. "During the night, I moved the body toward the outer area, beyond town. I planned my route to avoid all cameras and surveillance drones. I laid him where we'd 'find' him the next day and returned home to rest."

Isaac scowled at him. "I bet you couldn't sleep."

General Johnson rubbed his neck. "Not a wink. The guilt kept me up all night."

Isaac nodded. "Proper actions lead to restful sleep."

The General sighed. "The next morning, I met with Senator Pennell and the lead agent while running on fumes. I suggested searching the area where I'd left the body, knowing full well we hadn't looked there yet. Later that morning, we got word they had found him."

Isaac scoffed. "All according to plan."

General Johnson cleared his throat. "Senator Pennell broke into tears. By the afternoon, they had recovered his remains."

He shook his head. "I was ready to throw them a few low-level terrorists as scapegoats. Then, an agent mentioned drone footage they'd gotten."

Isaac narrowed his eyes. "I thought you avoided all cameras and drones."

"So did I." The General whispered. "My heart dropped into the pit of my stomach."

He took a deep breath. "I did not assign aircraft to the area. My conviction would come from the tech I kidnapped someone to get. A person died because I tried to do the right thing the wrong way, and I was ready to pay for it. I had accepted my fate."

Isaac extended a hand, palm up. "So how is it you're sitting here with me today?"

General Johnson sat forward. "When they launched the hologram, the body appeared where I had left it. Then, someone walked into the scene. They rotated the recording, and we all saw who it was. The lead agent."

Isaac shook his head. "That's not possible."

The General nodded. "I know, but I restrained him and had him escorted out by other agents. He claimed innocence the entire time, as he should have."

General Johnson looked Isaac in the eye. "Senator Pennell grasped my hand and thanked me for catching the man responsible for his son's death. I told him bringing the killer to justice was my pleasure."

Isaac frowned. "Why would you do that?"

The General leaned back. "What choice did I have? I used the opportunity presented to me."

He paused. "Senator Pennell then led me to meet the friend who had recommended me for the job. We walked into another office, and that's when I met Mr. White. The Senator introduced us, then left to break the news to his wife. Mr. White pointed to a chair, puffed his cigar, glanced at me and said, 'Always check for cameras before you dump a body.' "

Isaac shook his head. "How did he know you moved the remains?"

General Johnson gestured upward. "He told me Jack Lincoln was the manufacturing partner for my drones. Mr. White kept control of one, claiming it was to watch over me. For my protection."

Isaac leaned forward. "Why did he believe you needed protection?"

The General gazed through the window. "The lead agent had questioned my decisions, where we searched and where we didn't. I asked him how long he had known about the Senator's son. He responded, 'For weeks.' and puffed on his cigar. Then he asked me, 'Who do you think killed him?'.".

Isaac held up his hands. "Mr. White had Senator Pennell's child murdered?"

General Johnson nodded. "He claimed he was protecting me."

Isaac shook his head. "Why would he kill his friend's kid to protect you?"

The General folded his arms. "Mr. White mentioned that if I hadn't disobeyed orders and followed my instincts, President Mary Jackson would be dead. He told me the Senator wasn't a friend, just an acquaintance. A useful tool. But in me, he saw potential."

He grabbed the window ledge. "Mr. White offered me the Deputy Director position at The Agency, claiming our collective efforts would surpass Pennell's contribution to the continents. He said that Senator Pennell was too corrupt and too blinded by personal ambitions, but I was committed to my mission."

Isaac crossed his arms. "Is that why he forged the hologram?"

General Johnson nodded. "Mr. White gave me a choice, serve as his second-in-command and keep hunting threats to the continents, or he'd show Senator Pennell the unaltered recording. I shook his hand and accepted."

He sighed. "A few months ago, Senator Pennell came to The Agency and asked Mr. White and me to revisit his son's disappearance. When Mr. White questioned why, the Senator said the lead agent had continued to insist on his innocence, and he believed him. Mr. White told him we'd investigate it."

The General's voice grew quieter. "Senator Pennell smiled, clasped our hands, and turned to leave. As he reached for the door, Mr. White slammed his head against it. The Senator fell to the floor. Mr. White climbed on top of him and strangled him to death."

Isaac's eyes widened as General Johnson stared out the window.

Isaac shook his head. "What did you do?"

The General turned back to Isaac. "I panicked. Mr. White leaned out the door and told his assistant to send in the cleaners. Two agents came in and took Senator Pennell's body for disposal. Once they left, I asked why he did it. He said the Senator would've become a threat to me, and I was too valuable to lose over a disposable tool."

Isaac frowned. "So, you had a pleasant chat with the devil, who knew all your sins. He killed an innocent young man, and you shook his hand and went into business with him. Then he kills Senator Pennell."

He pointed at General Johnson. "You understood from the beginning how ruthless he was. Why not leave The Agency when he murdered the Senator? Why tell this to me now?"

Tears welled in the General's eyes. "The answer to all your questions is my wife, Shelley. She died at the hands of terrorists. The same ones I stopped from assassinating the President."

He cried. "They targeted her because their leader's wife and seven-year-old daughter perished when I redirected the missile strike they sent to kill President Jackson to where I believed he was hiding."

General Johnson wiped the tears away. "After that, I grew obsessed with hunting him down and eliminating every group that threatened any citizen of the United Continents of America."

He slammed his fist onto the seat. "My mission and vision were so clear. Senator Pennell's interference presented an obstruction that required removal."

The General stared straight ahead. "Kidnapping his son wasn't how I should've handled the situation. I've made a lot of poor decisions that I need to make amends for since Shelley died. For all my actions and inactions. I must be the person she was proud to marry. The man her love helped shape. Not the cold mercenary I have become."

He looked down at the floor. "I saw how Andrea stared at me. That hurt. It reminded me of Shelley, and how she'd look at me the same way now."

General Johnson peered at Isaac. "The best time to change was months ago. The next ideal moment is this instant. It is never too late to transform into the person I should have become. There's still time to fix this. I intend to dedicate the rest of my life to making amends. If you give me my arm back, I'll fight by your side against Mr. White."

Isaac shook his head. "Your story about Shelley is touching, maybe even moving. But you tried to kill me, my son, and the others. Because of that, I don't trust you. I never will. It's hard to trust a man who shakes your hand, smiles in your face, and then tries to murder your kid two days later."

The General nodded. "I understand I wronged you and Liam, and in doing so, I betrayed Brian and the love he had for both of you. For that, I'm sorry. I just hope I can earn your trust again. In the fight ahead, you'll want me at your side when Mr. White makes his next move."

Chapter Eleven

Colonel Brian piloted the Hovercopter to The Agency with Emily in the copilot's seat, gazing out the window.

The buildings below stood unlit, illuminated by the red light emitted from the forcefield. The snow covering the rooftops reflected the distinct glow of the dome.

He gently tapped her arm. "Ever since the mission in the United Middle East, I've had a tough time remembering your mother as vividly as I want. People I see regularly, I can remember just fine. But the ones I haven't seen in a while... they're blurry. And the folks I've not seen in years, I forget. I hadn't laid eyes on your mom in a long while."

Brian pulled out a folded piece of paper. "Whenever a clear recollection of her comes back to me, I write it down. I examine old photos of her and this note every morning. Technology can fail, and I never wanted to risk forgetting her again. I'd rather view faded photographs than let her memory slip away. The more I look at this, the more I remember."

He handed the paper to Emily.

She unfolded it and read aloud:

I first became acquainted with her during my time as a soldier; she worked under Isaac and possessed remarkable beauty. My wife consistently encouraged my personal and professional growth and brought levity to my life. She was exceptionally compassionate and dedicated to her principles.

Emma provided steadfast support, and together we raised a wonderful daughter.

Emily teared up as she turned to Brian.

Colonel Brian took her hand. "I just added that last part before we departed."

He paused. "I'm so sorry for what I did to push you away. My condition has improved. I want to make up for the hurt I caused you."

She cupped his hand between hers. "It's okay, Dad. I forgive you. But I haven't forgiven myself for running. You needed me, and I left you alone. I can't forgive myself for staying distant or not coming back sooner. I'm mad at myself for being home and not seeing you until the world is ending."

Brian gently squeezed her lower hand. "It's alright, Emily. I forgive you. And I love you."

She smiled. "I love you too, Dad."

Emily hesitated. "Can you remember what happened on that mission?"

He shook his head. "I try, but I can't recall anything. The whole event is fuzzy. I've read the reports, and nothing seems out of place. We defeated the bad guys and came home. But the strange part is that whenever I ask anyone about it, they avoid details. Everyone rushes through the conversation. It makes me wonder if I did something I'd rather not remember."

She shook her head. "You? Doing anything like that? I don't believe it. You're the best man I've ever known."

Colonel Brian smiled. "You are right. Perhaps I am just eager to recall, and not knowing is making me anxious."

Emily nodded and turned her seat toward him. "When this situation is over, we should visit Mom's grave together."

He looked down, then shook his head. "I... I can't do that."

She frowned. "Why not?"

His eyes welled with tears. "It hurts to be there. Seeing her name on a gravestone, knowing Emma's gone... not having her with me every day. Remembering her the way I do in life is easier. It's preferable to reliving the moment she... died."

Emily placed a hand on his shoulder. "I understand. Those first visits were tough for me as well. But now when I go, I talk to her. I know she's listening from Heaven, and I always feel good when I leave. You've only been once since the funeral. Going back could help you confront what you've been evading. Talking to her might even bring forth more memories. Maybe getting through this emotional wall is what your mind needs."

She gently squeezed his hand. "Mom would wish for you to move on and be happy. She wouldn't want you stuck in sadness, mourning her for years. If we honor and remember the ones we've lost, there's no shame in living fully with the time we have."

Brian nodded. "You're right, Em. After this mission is over... we'll go. I'll go. That is exactly what I need."

He turned to her. "When did I raise such a smart and caring daughter?"

Emily smiled. "When you weren't looking. I watched how you and Mom lived, and I wanted to be like both of you."

Colonel Brian shook his head. "You will be better than us. That's all I've always desired, for you to surpass our efforts. To live a fuller, happier life. To get married, have kids, and be a greater parent than we were. To raise even better children."

He smiled warmly. "You could become one of history's greatest people. I believe that."

She stood, walked over and hugged him. "I love you, Dad."

Brian held her tightly with an arm. "I love you too."

Emily sat back in her seat. Her smile faded into horror as she stared straight ahead.

She pointed. "Daddy... look."

His voice was tight. "You guys might want to see this."

Isaac and General Johnson rushed to the cockpit.

Below them, thousands of Taken were advancing toward The Agency.

Chapter Twelve

James held Jess in his arms as they flew through the underground tunnels known as The Web. They sped through the lit cement passage toward General Johnson's office on the North Side. Robert soared ahead in his Warlock Armor, with Liam speeding out in front of him.

Jessica glanced at James and saw the focus etched on his face. She leaned in and kissed him on the lips.

He smiled, eyes still on the way forward. "What was that for?"

She returned his smile. "For the time we lost. And for you being a hero."

James chuckled. "What do you mean?"

Jess giggled. "What do I mean? All of this. Everything you've done. You fought the Taken, stood up to the General, protected us from the Pallid, and then jumped out a window after Robby. That was the bravest thing I've ever seen. What happened in that moment?"

He looked at her, his expression turning serious. "I had no time to think; I just reacted. I wasn't positive if I could save him, but I knew I had to try. When I leaped, I tucked my arms to my sides to fall faster."

James shook his head. "It was the scariest moment of my life. I wasn't scared of dying; I was afraid of failing to protect my son. When he reached out to me, I wasn't certain I'd get to him in time. I didn't know whether either of us would make it. Or if you'd lose us both."

He thought about the fear etched on his son's face. "But then, by God's grace, my powers activated at the last second. I sped up, caught him, and pulled up right before we hit the ground."

James exhaled. "When we landed, Rob gave me the biggest hug he's ever given me. He thanked me and told me he loved me."

James smiled. "Robby said I was his superhero."

Jess beamed in return. "I mean, we are flying, and Liam is running super fast."

He chuckled. "I guess we are superheroes. I told him to hop on my back, and he said, 'Go kick ass.' So that's what I did."

She kissed him on the cheek. "I was so scared when you jumped out the window. I thought I'd endured so many trials, fought so hard to get to you, but then lost you and Robby. It devastated me. Then you rose with him ... it was an incredible sight."

James frowned. "Being a superhero doesn't matter if we don't win. If I saved him only to lose him in the end. If I found you just to lose you again..."

Jessica kissed him once more.

He smiled. "I'm already getting used to this again."

She touched his lips with two fingers. "We will not fail. Four of you have powers. Robby has a flying suit of armor. I have protective gear that lets me pack a punch. Isaac is an officer, and Brian's a trained soldier. The General might even prove trustworthy."

Jess smiled. "Every single one of us has something or someone to fight for. Nothing will stop our group from protecting each other."

James grinned at her. "How can I argue with that optimism?"

She shook her head. "You can't."

They both chuckled.

She gripped him tighter. "After this situation is done, you, Robby and I need to go on vacation."

He nodded. "That's a great idea."

James shifted from flying to hovering, and they landed at the entrance of General Johnson's office, right next to Robert.

Liam stood with his back against the doorway. "Took you long enough."

James chuckled as he walked up the steps. "Sorry for making you wait two seconds."

Liam shook his head. "When you're this fast, two seconds feels the same as two minutes."

James smiled. "Let's unlock the door Liam."

He and Liam entered the General's and Colonel's codes, and the door slid open. They stepped into the office. Papers were scattered across the desk, and someone had left the drawers ajar.

James glanced around. "Looks like someone's been here recently."

Liam looked at him. "You think it was Sofia and Andrea? Or Mateo?"

James shook his head. "I'm not sure. The question is, what were they hoping to find?"

He turned to Jess and Robert. "Alright, look for anything useful. We'll need every advantage when we reach The Agency. We must stop Mateo and Mr. White, so everything might help in the fight ahead."

They all nodded and moved to different parts of the office.

Robert's search came up empty, so he consulted the instruction sheet for the Warlock armor. He converted his Microbot Cape into a weapon. The cloak shortened as excess Microbots crawled up his shoulders and down his right arm, forming into a sword in his hand.

Robert held it up. "Look at this Dad."

James turned, studied his blade, and smiled. "That's pretty cool."

Liam slow-clapped. "Show me one more impressive thing about that suit, and I'll peel you out of it like a tuna can."

Everyone laughed.

James and Jess continued searching.

Liam glanced around. "What? I was being serious."

James searched under the desk and noticed a hidden compartment underneath the top. He pressed the corners, and it swung open.

James smiled. "These might come in handy."

Liam turned with interest. "What? I wanna see. Show me."

James stood up, holding two triple-black glossy pistols.

Liam grinned. "Those are badass. Did you find any ammo with them?"

James shook his head as he inspected the weapons. "No, and there doesn't seem to be a place to load rounds."

Liam frowned. "What? That makes no sense."

James pointed at the back. "There's a button to switch firing modes... and another button here."

Liam held out his hand. "Let me see one."

James handed over a pistol. Liam aimed at the wall to the left and pulled the trigger. They all gasped as an ice bullet struck the surface and exploded on impact, freezing everything it touched.

James and Liam stared at each other in awe.

Liam switched to full-auto firing mode while James fired in semi-automatic. Then James pressed the second button. This time, the frozen projectile stuck in the wall without exploding.

Liam glowered at James. "Alright, now I really dislike the General. How dare he have infinite-ammo ice pistols and not put them to use? Worse than that, he didn't let ME use them."

James laughed as Liam handed the pistol back. "I don't know. These are cool."

He gave the guns to Jessica. "You should take these."

She eyed them with doubt. "What about you guys?"

Robert raised his hand. "Yeah, what about us guys?"

James smiled. "Liam and I have superpowers, and you have the Warlock armor. You can make any weapon you want."

Robby lowered his hand.

James continued. "Jess could use these to keep a distance between her and the Taken or the Pallid."

He turned to her. "Setting two, the right button, is for creatures. And setting one freezes humans. Choose the firing mode you prefer. You need these more than anyone, especially since they match your outfit."

She smiled. "When you put it like that, how can I say no?"

James grinned. "You can't."

Liam stepped toward him. "We should move."

James nodded and turned to face the faux wall. "Okay, I don't think there's anything else here for us. Let's get to The Agency."

Robert and Jessica nodded.

James and Liam focused their powers, generating protective energy layers around themselves.

James took Robert and Jess's hands and created individual shields to protect them.

Robby touched her shoulder, and Microbots crawled up her neck and face, forming a facemask. From her cheekbones to her hairline, the tiny robots turned transparent.

He also surrounded the group with hovering minuscule robots.

James lifted the wall, and they exited into the office area.

After stepping onto the streets of Dead City, Robert's robots scattered the nearby Remnant.

Liam took off toward Lemon Station. Robert sent Microbots with him and left a few behind for James and Jess before flying after Liam.

James held her close and soared away.

Once they arrived at the terminal, they scanned their surroundings. They saw no movement and entered with caution.

After surveying the platform, James walked over to the tracks. "Well, the train is gone."

Liam grinned. "Finally, I get to test my speed."

He dropped into a sprinter's stance.

James held out a hand. "Wait. I want to make sure everyone's okay after going through the Remnant."

Liam shook his head. "Between our energy shields, the shot we got, her immunity, and Robert's Microbots, we're fine. Look at the little guys; they're still active. You check on them while I scout ahead, okay?"

Before James could respond, Liam was gone with a cloud of dust, swirling Remnant, and a squeal of joy.

He turned to Robert and Jess. "How about you two? Are you okay?"

They nodded.

James patted his son on the shoulder. "The floating Microbots were a smart idea. The helmet for Jess, an even smarter one."

Robby smiled. "Thanks Dad. I know we're all supposedly protected from the Remnant, but better safe than sorry."

James nodded, then felt a gust of wind behind him and turned.

Liam pointed down the tunnel. "The Pallid have Sofia and Andrea surrounded. We've got to go now."

He took off running. James carried Jessica as he flew, with Robert close behind. They all pushed themselves to their limits.

As James soared next to Robert, he tapped his arm. "Make sure she stays safe. You two stay back. We'll handle most of them."

Robert shook his head. "I can help, Dad. Look at this suit. I can protect Jess; and more. Besides, she can take care of herself."

James shook his head. "You can, but I want you both to shoot from a distance. This isn't about holding you back; it's strategy. Watch each other's backs."

They both nodded.

As they landed at the train station under The Agency, a massive horde swarmed the platform. Red flashing lights bathed the area in a harsh glow. James glanced toward the elevator just in time to see the doors close with Andrea and Sofia inside.

Jessica turned to him. "You need all the help you can get. Let Robby fight with you. I can protect myself, and I'll call out if I need a hand."

James gave her a concerned look. "Are you sure? You were gone for a year. I don't want to risk losing you again."

She moved toward him, and her face covering receded as she kissed him. "You won't lose me again, I promise."

The facemask reformed over her mouth. James nodded.

He turned to Liam and Robert. "Alright. Let's get this done."

They both nodded. Liam sprinted into the fray while Robert soared above the horde. The Microbots on his palms sparked with green electricity, and he unleashed a rapid-fire volley of lightning blasts from his hands.

James flew Jess onto the train car. Jess pulled out her twin black Ice Pistols and started shooting.

Liam darted through the mass, weaving between enemies and striking them down with quick punches.

James shot up to the top of the station, then rocketed down to the ground. His landing hit with such force that it knocked down every Pallid within a ten-foot radius, and Liam.

Liam sprang to his feet. "Thanks for that."

He held out his hand. "Rob, make me a hatchet."

Robert's Microbots assembled into a blade, and he tossed it to Liam.

The pale ones turned their attention to James and rushed him. He punched one aside, grabbed a second, and hurled it into a cluster. A creature lunged at him. He caught it by the throat and slammed it onto the floor. Another jumped at him from behind. James spun and delivered a crushing kick.

Robert swooped through a crowd of Pallid and leveled them with a clothesline. Liam finished each creature that tried to rise with his Microbot Hatchet.

Meanwhile, a group of undead surrounded the HoverTrain car where Jess stood. One leaped at her. She dropped onto her back and shot it mid-air as it passed over her.

James landed beside the train car. He pressed his hands together and formed a growing ball of energy. As soon as the Pallid group noticed him, James launched the energy beam straight at them. It ripped through the remaining creatures, blasting open a hole in the station's cement wall opposite the elevator. "Don't mess with my fiancée."

He scanned for more enemies, but none remained.

Liam raced over to the elevator. Robert landed beside him. James turned to Jess. She smiled as he wrapped his arms around her and flew over to join the others.

Liam looked at James. "Someone broke the controls. I've pressed it thousands of times, and the elevator still hasn't come."

James smirked. "Thousands of times?"

Liam frowned. "You don't believe me? Watch."

He rapidly jabbed the button with precision until James raised his eyebrows in surprise.

James chuckled. "Okay, okay, I believe you. Just stop before you wear your finger down to a nub."

He looked around. "There must be another way to call it. Andrea and Sofia were on it a moment ago."

Everyone searched the area surrounding the elevator, but low, guttural roars interrupted them.

They pivoted toward the tunnel on the right as more Pallid emerged.

Without hesitation, James turned back and ripped the elevator doors apart with his hands. Inside, the shaft glowed red from warning lights along the center, with white beacons outlining the corners.

Robert flew up the shaft while Liam sprinted up the wall. James grabbed Jess and ascended after them.

Near the top, Robby reached the underside of the elevator. He opened the service hatch, and they entered.

James forced the elevator doors open and saw two women ready to fight. Andrea and Sofia stood poised to strike, energy swirling around their hands.

Isaac and Colonel Brian stood behind with their pistols drawn.

Emily and General Johnson were further back.

She ran to Liam and hugged him. Sofia walked over and embraced both James and Robert.

James turned to Isaac. "Have you found Mr. White yet?"

Isaac shook his head. "We all just got here. A swarm of Taken surrounded the upstairs entrance."

Sofia nodded. "We had to fight through a group of Pallid to reach the elevator. I'm guessing you beat the next wave if you came that direction."

James nodded. "We did, and more were coming right after. Now it looks like we'll be fighting again. Hopefully, for the last time."

Sofia pointed to the camera above them. "On the way up, Mr. White's hologram appeared. He's expecting us."

James gave a wry smile. "Then we shouldn't disappoint him. The quicker we stop him and Mateo, the sooner we can undo the last forty-eight hours. Let's move."

He stepped forward, and the rest followed.

Behind them, the Pallid began climbing up the elevator shaft, stacking on top of one another as they rose.

Chapter Thirteen

They moved through The Agency's lab toward Mr. White's office. The main lights were off, so James led them by the pulsing red warning beacons.

No scientists shouted or rushed around the laboratory. No agents lurked between workstations or stood guard by the elevator. Only the echo of their footsteps broke the silence.

No one was in the lab.

Liam glanced at James. "Where is everybody?"

James scanned the empty laboratory. "I don't know."

They continued down the main hallway toward the operatives' side of the facility. Still, no one was in sight. Passing between rows of desks, they headed straight for Mr. White's office.

At the door, Isaac eased it open and stepped inside. Liam and Colonel Brian followed, with James bringing up the rear. The room was empty.

Isaac glanced at Liam. "Where do you think he is?"

Liam's gaze drifted toward the doorway. "He has to be close."

Mr. White's hologram appeared. "I'll show you where I am. Waiting for you to find me wastes valuable time."

With a mechanical hum, the back wall of the office slid upward.

Liam smirked at the projection. "I take it hidden rooms were all the rage when you built this place and every one of your offices?"

The image vanished, revealing a long metal wall with a glass window stretching from end to end, and a door. Beyond it lay a tall room with metallic walls and a gleaming black tile floor. In the dim light, Mr. White stood beside two towering eight-foot machines.

Liam ran to the entrance and yanked the handle. It didn't budge.

Mr. White raised a finger. "You'll walk through that door only when I allow it."

James stepped forward. "Are you responsible for the forcefield?"

Mr. White nodded.

James shook his head. "So, you trap innocent people with the Taken and the Pallid, knowing they'll turn? That's not saving anyone. You are making the problem worse."

Mr. White extended his hand. "You're seeing a corner of the canvas. Stand with me, and I'll show you the whole picture."

James narrowed his eyes. "I don't join men who slaughter cities and call it vision."

Everyone except General Johnson shook their heads.

Mr. White chuckled. "Ultimately, you will be beside me. And when that day comes, you'll see that I'm the hero of this story."

Liam twirled a finger beside his head. "Yeah, and they'll label you insane."

Mr. White's smile sharpened. "They called the dreamers deranged too. They built the world to which you cling. The meek protect what is now. What's next will be redefined by the bold."

His gaze locked on James. "I'm not crazy. My perspective allows me to observe things from a greater distance. I recognize the path to survival. With me, we won't just save the world... we'll perfect it."

James shook his head. "Then prove it. Help us stop Mateo and face justice. Otherwise, you're not the hero of this story; you are its biggest threat."

Mr. White scoffed. "Mateo will never help you. Am I the only one here who sees what he has become?"

His gaze swept over them. "You know what he is? A monster. Do you believe an appeal to his past humanity will reach him? Face the truth about who you're dealing with, and you'll understand how to stop him."

Andrea stepped forward, pointing at him. "You made him this way. If he's a monster, that makes you his creator. He wouldn't have gone down this path if you hadn't tried to murder us."

Mr. White shook his head. "I never attempted to kill you. Only him. I perceived your potential and believed you could serve The Agency. But him? I knew what lay just under the surface. The fiend you refused to see. I recognized the rage. Because I carry it myself. I mastered mine; he wanted to unleash his. It was apparent from his expression. I won't apologize. If I'd succeeded, we wouldn't be in this mess."

He turned to Colonel Brian. "If you want to talk about my humanity, look no further than your trusted ally. Brian is proof of my love for life. He perished on a mission two years ago, and my scientists resurrected him. Brian died a second time, and they brought him back again."

Emily's eyes snapped to her dad. "What do you mean, you brought him back twice? How is that even possible?"

Mr. White pointed to the veins in his wrist. "Technology and DNA. He wasn't the father you remembered. That Brian looked like him, but did you notice his memory slips... and his erratic behavior?"

Emily nodded. "Why?"

He sighed. "That's the result of an imprinting process I call Project Rebirth. A lab-grown body in his image with a digital psyche implant. The clone whose cognitive function and conduct faltered was a generation-one model. The man standing before you is from Generation Two. Given time, those issues should resolve."

Colonel Brian chuckled. "You're insane. I haven't died twice. More lies. Where's the proof?"

Mr. White turned to General Johnson. "Shall I show him and his daughter, or will you tell him yourself?"

All eyes shifted to the General.

He met Mr. White's gaze, then looked at Brian. "It's true. It happened during our mission two years ago to stop the United Terrorists Against America. After we diverted the missile from the President, a terrorist, who wasn't as dead as we thought, shot you in the stomach. I killed him, but I couldn't save you."

General Johnson's voice thickened. "I held you as you died. I wouldn't leave you there. We rushed you back to The Agency. When we join, we all undergo digital psyche mapping. Weekly psych evaluations update thought patterns, improve processing, and make us better soldiers and agents. They also flag negative changes."

Mr. White stepped forward. "As soon as I got word from the General, I put my best scientists on saving Brian."

Colonel Brian shook his head. "I remember dying a couple of days ago. Why can't I recall passing away two years back?"

Mr. White tapped his temple. "We thought erasing your first death from your psyche would be merciful. But trauma isn't erasable, only concealable. Your mind tried to tell you the truth, which caused the erratic behavior. Changing one memory disrupts others. That was the source of your instability. The second time, we overwrote your original passing with the recent event."

Isaac pounded on the glass. "Why would you do that to him? If you knew about the issues, why would you endanger Emily? Why not tell him the truth?"

Mr. White stepped closer. "Sometimes knowing the facts isn't what we need. I never meant to put her in danger. I did not intend to cause harm to my niece."

Colonel Brian stared at him. "What do you mean your niece?"

Mr. White fixed his gaze on Brian. "We share the same father, different mothers. His mother was our father's wife; my mom was his lover. When he refused to leave her, my mother took me away. I never saw him again. I was a baby and have no memory of him. Three years ago, my mom told me I had a brother, just before she died. When I discovered his line of work, I planned to recruit him... and get to know him."

He hesitated. "I was waiting for the right moment to tell you. This isn't ideal, but I have limited time."

Colonel Brian shook his head. "I don't believe you."

Mr. White projected a hologram of himself, Brian, and their father. "You don't have to trust me. Facts speak for themselves. Look at the DNA results."

Colonel Brian stared at the ninety-nine percent relation probability. "Why didn't you tell me when I first arrived? Why not earlier? When would have been the 'right time'?"

Mr. White nodded. "You're right. I should have disclosed it at the beginning. For that, I am sorry. But we may discuss this later. We have more pressing issues. I'm asking you again. Join me and help save the world. There's more at stake than you realize, and I have a plan to fix it."

James stepped forward. "If so much is on the line and you have a plan, then share it with us so we can make an informed decision."

Mr. White shook his head. "I'll only reveal my plan to the committed and loyal. You've already proven to be a hindrance these past few days. That will have to change. If you won't join me, my plan stays within my circle of need-to-know for now. You'll be by my side in the end. Of that, I'm sure."

General Johnson pointed at him. "You helped Mateo hunt down the terrorists. Because you gave him a lab, he made the Taken. You tried, and didn't kill him, and as a result he's unleashed this on us. This is your attempt to clean up the mess you made."

Mr. White shook his head. "When we first met, you were a broken man. I provided your sorrow direction, and your purpose focus. You excelled in your work. Until cybernetics and emotions started interfering. Too much hardware, too fast. Cyberpsychosis is clouding your judgment."

General Johnson looked at Andrea. "It's not Cyberpsychosis. I realized Shelley would be ashamed of who I've become."

He turned back to Mr. White. "I'm no longer the person she loved. That guy wouldn't have stopped looking for his missing daughter, even after exhausting every lead. That's what I need to do. Somewhere along the way, I lost sight of what mattered most. Family and honor."

Mr. White straightened his tie. "What if I told you they were both living, and I could take you to them? Would you join me then?"

The General's face flushed red. "They're alive? You knew, and you didn't tell me?!"

Mr. White cleared his throat. "Follow me, and I'll clarify everything."

General Johnson slammed his right fist against the glass. "You'll explain now, or I will kill you."

Mr. White scowled. "I offer you what you've lost, and your first response is to threaten me?"

He leaned closer. "So be it. Come in and kill me."

The door slid open, and Mr. White gestured him forward.

The General turned to Isaac. "Please give me my arm back."

Isaac scanned the group for objections. Finding none, he glanced between General Johnson and the cybernetic limb before handing it to him. The General locked it into the port in his shoulder on the left, then strode through the doorway. The others followed close behind.

General Johnson closed the distance, boots striking the floor like war drums. At ten feet away, Mr. White tapped his HoloWatch.

The General collapsed onto his left side.

Mr. White reddened. "When the missile you fired at Andrea turned on you, I spared your life. I didn't leave you half a man. The team installed innovative cybernetics and a spinal gyroscope to help with balance. Just now, I switched it off. You think those limbs are yours? They're mine. I sought only loyalty in exchange. What have you given me since then? Nothing but defiance."

General Johnson shook with rage. "I don't need your toys to kill you. I'll still end you with one arm and leg."

The General struggled to his feet under the weight of the cybernetics and glared at Mr. White. "You should've reunited me with my family. You didn't. That isn't loyalty; that's betrayal. And for that, you'll die."

Mr. White sighed. "Death comes for most, Oliver. Some of us, however, may never meet it. You unfortunately aren't one of them."

General Johnson used every ounce of strength to dash at him.

Mr. White snapped his fingers. The General's body went limp, his last breath escaping in a ragged exhale.

Andrea's scream tore through the room.

Chapter Fourteen

James stared at General Johnson's lifeless body sprawled across the glossy black tiles. His eyes lifted to Mr. White, who stood calm. "You killed him."

Mr. White nodded. "Yes. The General could have been part of the solution, but he refused to give me the chance to prove it."

He pointed at James. "You don't have to repeat his mistake. Let me show you how we can still save this world."

Colonel Brian rose from General Johnson's side, his hand near his weapon. "Why? Why do this, and how?"

Mr. White exhaled. "I didn't want to, but he left me no choice. Threats only lead to more chaos, and I will not allow that. As for how, thank Mateo and Andrea. After the failed attempt on Mateo's life, I recovered the Evolution formula from The Agency's servers. My scientists recreated it, and I consumed it."

Liam scratched his head. "If you've got powers now, why do you even need us?"

Mr. White pointed to his HoloWatch. "Because time is against me. The formula I took wasn't the authentic version; it was a deception. It granted me power, yes, but it's also killing me. Only Mateo and Andrea know the actual equation."

Andrea shook her head. "I don't know the formula. While he worked on it, I was still recovering from my transformation. Only Mateo knows it.

And even if I did, I wouldn't give it to you. You do not deserve power, or life, after all you've done."

Mr. White sighed. "I'm sorry you feel that way. But understand this, if I die or fail alone, we all perish. If you stand with me and I fall, you'll still have the chance to save those who remain."

James crossed his arms. "Save them from what? The Taken? The Pallid? Or you?"

Mr. White gave a casual shrug. "Rescue them from it all. I don't care how, only that the citizens of the United Continents of America survive. That's the only goal that matters."

James pointed to General Johnson's body. "If it's all about saving people, why kill him? Why eliminate someone who could've helped?"

Mr. White's gaze lingered on Oliver. "I thought the same. With his record, his mind, his enhancements; he should've been invaluable. But he threatened me, and in doing so, imperiled everyone. I can't allow failure. So now, you five are pivotal to the future."

James frowned. "Don't you mean the four of us?"

Mr. White's lips curved in a knowing smile. "No. I meant what I said."

James shielded Robert. "If you think I'll let you use my son, you're dead wrong."

Mr. White chuckled. "Not him. I wasn't talking about him."

He pointed straight at Jessica. "I was referring to her."

James froze, following the line of his hand. "Jess?"

His voice caught. "What do you mean?"

Sofia stepped forward, confusion in her tone. "Earlier, when you told the General to bring you 'the women,' I thought you meant me and my mother."

Mr. White's eyes never left Jessica. "No, Sofia. I choose my words carefully. She's far more important than you realize."

Jess staggered back a step, her face draining of color. "Me? No... no, that's impossible."

Her hands trembled as she shook her head. "Why me?"

Mr. White only smiled.

James' fists flared with energy. "What makes her so special?"

Mr. White gave a faint smile. "Your hands tell me you already know. But let me remind you of the General lying dead at your feet. The friend I killed. So don't do something foolish."

Blue energy surged across James' body. "I want you to say it."

Mr. White adjusted his tone, measured and unhurried. "If you insist. Jessica has been in my facility since the terrorist attack last year."

James launched himself forward. Mr. White tapped his HoloWatch. A white forcefield shimmered, encompassing him, along with the two machines beside him. James struck it hard, and it threw him back onto the floor.

Mr. White lifted a hand, steady and unflinching. "Why come at me? You should thank me."

James staggered to his feet, his voice raw with rage. "Thank you? I believed she was dead! Losing her destroyed me. I mourned her for nine months. Nine months! Because you took her from me right before our wedding. And you want me to thank you?!"

Mr. White nodded. "Yes. Your reaction is selfish."

James stepped closer, fists blazing, his glare burning through the shimmering barrier. "Give me one reason I shouldn't end your life the moment I get the chance."

Mr. White smiled. "I'll offer you a trio of reasons. One, the world needs me to save it. You may have the powers, James, but you lack the reasoning. Two, you can't kill me. You'd wind up like General Johnson whenever I decide. And then what happens to Robert and Jessica? Three, the vaccine I created to protect you from the Remnant came from her blood."

All eyes snapped to Jess. James turned back to Mr. White, his jaw tightening, shoulders trembling with restrained energy.

Mr. White leaned against one of the machines. "So yes, I took your fiancée and kept her here. However, because of that, I have a vaccine that provides protection from the Remnant, perhaps even more."

James said nothing, but his fists glowed, curling tighter as his breath came sharp through his nose.

Mr. White extended a hand. "I've told you many times, I am not the villain of this story. I'm the hero. If I must walk this path alone, I will. But the more help I have, the safer your family shall be."

Jess stepped up to the forcefield, fury flashing in her eyes. "Fuck you. You stole a year from us, and now you want our help? You're insane."

Mr. White shook his head. "He who sees all, perceives clearer than the rest. You don't know what's coming. I do. And I'm offering you a chance to become the heroes you pretend to be."

Liam moved to stand beside Jessica. "You've wronged everyone here. You claim to be the good guy, but you killed your friend, tried to kill us, and kidnapped Jess. Your hypocrisy is laughable. You aren't a hero; you're the villain. And we'll prove it when we stop you."

Mr. White chuckled. "I envy you, Liam. That level of ignorance must feel like bliss until the moment you miss your chance because you refuse to recognize it. As an officer, you only react. My role is to prevent a catastrophe before it happens. You're a responder; I'm a planner. We see the world differently, so our fates will always diverge. Enjoy your bliss while you can. Soon enough, it's going to turn to ash in your hands."

Mr. White studied them. "Though I may embody villainy, my every action, every awful deed, served a crucial purpose. You don't recognize it now, but you will. When the time comes, you'll follow me. The President sees it. Do you consider yourself more informed than her?"

Liam lifted a hand. "Let's not talk about politics."

Mr. White turned away. "Do you remember the failed assassination of the President six months ago?"

Liam nodded. "Who doesn't? They tried to kill her during a speech. One of her security agents jumped in front of her and took the bullet. What about it?"

Mr. White cleared his throat. "That try didn't fail. The shot passed through him and struck her. She died later that night in the Presidential House's private clinic."

He turned back and pointed at Brian. "Madam President Mary Jackson remains in office today because of the same process we created for him. She is the leader destined to guide the continents through these times. No matter how you feel about me, I made the world safer."

Liam shook his head. "I call that a failure. You didn't prevent her death. Brian died twice. You couldn't stop the terrorist attacks. And worst of all, you set things in motion that drove Mateo to unleash The Taken. Some planning skills. Did you think telling that story would tug at our hearts and make us side with you? Forget it. We'll never help you, never work for you, and never give you access to our powers."

Mr. White smiled. "Do you believe that's the only reason I want you to join me? It was part of it when I first asked, but it's no longer necessary. One of my agents, far more useful than I realized, stole a file from Mateo's lab. About a certain Chemical X. With that compound, we refined and hardened the Remnant. Refined Remnant powers these machines once thought only fiction. With them, we can save everyone. I don't need your powers for myself anymore. I seek your help for the world."

His smile collapsed. He looked past them.

The others turned and froze.

A figure stood in the darkness outside the doorway, hands clasped behind his back. Mateo's voice broke the silence. "Do not trust what he says. It's all lies, and I can prove it."

Chapter Fifteen

Everyone within the metal-walled chamber fixed their eyes on Mateo, who stood just inside the doorway, one step back from the threshold. Shadows veiled his face, but his blood-soaked right fist gleamed in the low light.

Mr. White's glare was cold. "You've looked better."

Mateo let out a soft chuckle. "Maybe. But I've never felt stronger."

Andrea started toward him.

He raised his dripping palm. "Stay where you are."

Mr. White extended his hand, his voice smooth. "What proof do you claim to have?"

Mateo's smile sharpened. "Indisputable evidence, courtesy of your old pal Jack Lincoln. You remember your business partner, right? I did you a favor by taking care of him. His death gave you full control of the companies and assets you now hold, you liar."

Mr. White chuckled. "Being a business partner isn't a crime. And as you said, you killed him. I had nothing to do with that."

Mateo nodded. "That's true. You didn't kill Jack; I did. I own that. But tell me, Mr. White... what have you omitted in your delusions of being the hero?"

Mr. White scowled. "I've shared what was necessary."

Mateo laughed, the sound sharp against the steel walls. "You haven't divulged everything they need to make an informed judgment. They've declined your offers more times than I can count, but I'll give them one last piece of information."

Mr. White's eyes narrowed. "Consider your next words. They may carry consequences greater than you realize."

Mateo's grin widened. "I've weighed the repercussions. I will have none."

With a flick of his HoloWatch, shimmering images lit the air. "This journal came from the Sparrow 2003 vault, hidden behind a painting in Jack Lincoln's office. He tucked it alongside the articles of incorporation and his last will. Jack clearly didn't trust you, Mr. White. He documented... certain activities. Activities the President, and the law, would condemn if they ever surfaced. Most of it doesn't concern this room, but one entry does."

He cleared his throat, and the holograms shifted into a slideshow of documents. "General Johnson intercepted chatter from the United Terrorists Against America about multiple coordinated strikes. Mr. White's plan was to use Jack Lincoln as an undercover agent. Posing as a crooked arms dealer, he convinced them that attacking several locations was too difficult."

Mateo looked at the group. "They armed them for one attack. He and Jack not only supplied the explosives but arranged their entry into the country. Once inside, the extremists changed targets because they no longer trusted Jack."

Jess's head snapped toward Mr. White. "You gave them weapons?"

He glared at Mateo, his voice cold. "The plan was to set a trap, to stop them before they could act. When they killed my surveillance team and shifted their target, everything unraveled."

Jess stepped forward, fire in her voice. "Unraveled? My three best friends died because of you!"

James shouted over his shoulder to Mateo; eyes still locked on Mr. White. "Did he give them the Remnant too?"

Mateo shook his head. "Nothing in Jack's journal mentioned that. But without Mr. White and Jack, terrorists would never have entered the country with that explosive. They're just as responsible for everything that followed as I am. If the U.T.A.A. hadn't bombed the station, I would never have started the research to save her or turned my rage against them. I own my actions. Do you, Mr. White?"

All eyes shifted to him. Mr. White clasped his hands behind his back, lifted his chin, and spoke with icy resolve. "I did what had to be done. We minimized the loss of life compared to what would have happened. After the attack, we trapped the terrorists within our borders to prosecute them. Life is full of decisions made in moments, hoping, but never knowing, how they'll play out. Unlike most people, I don't waste time mourning what-ifs. I can live with my choice far more than I could have lived with bombs ripping through the Capital, the Senate, the Department of Defense, the Department of Justice, and the stock market simultaneously."

He turned toward Jess, placing a hand over his chest, brows raised as though offering sincerity. "I am sorry for your losses. Innocents being hurt or killed always angers me. That choice proved preferable to destroying our leadership, protections, laws, and economy. The subway system was the most opulent in the world. An icon of capitalism, which proved to be a symbol they couldn't ignore. Its loss prevented more damage. Execution of their first plan would have resulted in a worse year, impacting more than Allegheny."

Jess shook her head, her voice hard. "A city overrun with Taken and Pallid is already the worst possible outcome. And being trapped inside this domed forcefield with them? You've sentenced every one of us to die."

Mr. White held up a finger. "Not everyone. I'm not dying today. And you don't have to either. No matter what you think of my methods, I deliver results. The result for you, James, Robert, and everybody else here might still be life."

Jess let out a bitter chuckle. "How many times must we tell you no? I'd rather die protecting the people in this dome than ever stand with you."

Mr. White sighed and shook his head. "Very well. If that's what you want, I can arrange it."

Mateo slammed his fist against the glass window beside him. The impact rattled the frame. "Enough!"

Every head turned as he stepped into the room. The sight of him drew collective gasps.

His face was corpse-pale with a swirling glow moving across his body.

His eyes reflected the light in unnatural hues, glowing bright against the darkness.

Sofia covered her mouth to stifle a cry.

Andrea staggered back a step, her voice trembling. "Teo... what happened to you?"

Mateo raised his left hand and rotated it in the dim light, examining the skin like an artifact. His fingertips ended in blackened nails, jagged and cracked, like obsidian. "After I escaped the research campus, I realized a bullet from Oliver had mortally wounded me. I had two choices: die in the gutter like an animal or risk consuming the unfinished Evolution formula."

He looked at Andrea. "I gambled and drank the vial. The completed formula brought Andrea back after death. I thought it might at least delay my own. But a Pallid snuck up and bit me as I drank it, fusing the compound and the infection. That bite was the catalyst. The spark."

He smiled, sharp and unhinged. "Behold the outcome. Not man, not monster. Something in between both. Half-Evolved, half-Pallid ... and all genius."

Liam leaned toward James. "If only it made him half humble too."

Andrea forced herself forward, her eyes never leaving his distorted face. "I... died? Why didn't you tell me? How long was I gone?"

Mateo's glow pulsed as he looked at her. "You were dead for three days. It seemed better if you remained unaware. I did not sleep, eat, or stop until I brought you back. And I succeeded."

Andrea's voice cracked as she stepped closer. "Let's fix this together."

Mateo raised his glowing hand again. "I don't want to fix this. I feel better than ever. Stronger than I've been in my life. And no one will take that from me. Not you, not Mr. White, not anyone here. I am the ultimate evolution. And you can't stop change."

Andrea's voice trembled. "Do you not see? You've become the very man you despised your entire life."

Mateo's gaze locked on Mr. White. "Sometimes the only way to fight power... is with more power."

Mr. White smiled at Mateo. "So, tell me then. What do you intend to do with all that power?"

Mateo leaned forward, his grin widening. "First, I'll kill you. Then we'll spread evolution across every continent."

He smirked. "It's already in motion."

Mr. White gave a short, dismissive laugh. "And how do you expect to kill me?"

Mateo's eyes glowed with satisfaction. "With help from my family."

Everyone looked at Sofia and Andrea.

Sofia shook her head.

He turned toward the office doors and swept his arms wide. Taken surged into the chamber. Reapers, a Hunter looming behind them, and an Evolved Thinker. Their unified roar reverberated through the chamber.

Before the echo faded, a flood of Pallid poured in behind them. They outnumbered the Taken three to one, their movements jerky, their eyes blazing with hunger. The two groups froze, facing each other, the air vibrating with snarls and the electric hum of imminent violence.

Mr. White tapped his HoloWatch. The doors sealed shut, trapping the creatures within. He arched a brow. "It seems both sides of your 'family' hate each other. As the saying goes, divided you fall."

More Taken and Pallid pressed against the glass walls, clawing and pounding in frustration. The chamber itself seemed to shrink, the sound of their fury rising like a storm.

Andrea's breath caught as her eyes fixed on the Evolved Thinker.

Mateo turned and smirked at Mr. White. "Kill them all."

For a heartbeat, nothing moved.

The room appeared to hold its breath. Taken crouched, muscles coiled, their claws scraping against the floor. The Pallid shuddered in place, their throats rumbling with inhuman growls. Even the glass walls trembled as if resisting the violence about to erupt.

Emily pressed her hand to her mouth. Robert prepared for action. Jess's knuckles whitened around the grip of her weapon.

Only Mr. White remained still, watching with a faint, inscrutable smile.

Then the first roar split the silence, deep, primal, unstoppable.

The chamber detonated into chaos.

Chapter Sixteen

James and the others stood in Mr. White's hidden chamber, flanked on both sides. Pallid pressed forward from the door to the steel wall. Taken stood across from them.

The Pallid surged. The Taken broke past James's group and hurled themselves at their enemies.

Mateo snapped his head toward Andrea. "What are you doing?"

Andrea's body blazed with energy. "What I should have done before you unleashed the Taken."

She shot forward, fist aimed at his chest. He slipped aside, seized her arm, and flung her into the wall. Andrea crumpled to the floor.

"Mom!" Sofia's cry tore through the chaos. She flared with her own energy, launched into the air, and drove a punch at Mateo. He swayed left, but Sofia twisted mid-flight, spinning into a brutal kick that cracked against his head and sent him crashing into the glass window.

James and Liam activated their energy.

Robert powered up his NanoSword.

Isaac, Brian, Emily, and Jess prepared their weapons and aimed at the Pallid swarm.

Mateo stood up while Andrea and Sofia continued their attack.

Liam sped among the Pallid, executing swift strikes, while James soared into the air and delivered forceful impacts to adversaries.

Robert moved through the fray, using his blade to neutralize opponents.

The Evolved Thinker's psychic shrieks kept the Hunter and Reapers in formation, pushing them against the Pallid.

A Pallid lunged from the side, seizing Jess. Its jaws snapped near her face as its fists struck her arms. Each strike sent a ripple of violet through her Echo bodysuit, the black fabric turning into glowing purple.

With a yell, Jessica unleashed her strength, slamming her fist into the creature's chest. The blow launched it across the chamber and into Mr. White's forcefield.

The purple light drained from her suit, fading back to black.

Mr. White watched the Pallid's body skid along the floor and bounce off the energy barrier. "This has gone on long enough."

He tapped his HoloWatch. A heavy clank echoed as a door slid open behind him. Two individuals entered together, holding hands. Every eye, Taken, Pallid, and human alike, snapped toward them.

As they drew closer, their forms came into view. Two unusual female Taken. Their skin was pitch-black; their bodies sculpted with corded muscle. One's hair burned a vivid red; the other's shimmered blue streaked with violet. Their faces appeared almost human at first, but when they smiled, rows of razor-sharp teeth emerged from splitting cheeks.

Mr. White's grin grew. "Meet the first of the Apexes. Fyre and Aion. My creation, perfected through the Reapers you were kind enough to bring me, and others we recovered."

The pair stood still, predators coiled in silence, giving chills.

Robert's eyes widened. "Dad, it's our neighbors from the stairs!"

Sofia turned to Andrea, her voice trembling. "He did it."

Mr. White extended his hand toward the group. His voice was steady and even. "Take out the targets."

Fyre and Aion smiled wider, teeth glinting in the light.

The Evolved Thinker unleashed the Hunter and half the blue Taken at the black Taken, sending the rest against the Pallid. Mateo countered, splitting some to the Taken, and the remainder toward the group.

Fyre lifted a hand as the Reapers and yellow Taken closed upon the Apexes. They froze mid-charge. Andrea spun towards the Evolved Thinker, who was edging backward. One by one, the Hunter and the blue Taken turned their heads to face her and the others.

Andrea glided over and grabbed Mateo by the collar. "Stop the Pallid from attacking us, and help."

He shook his head. "I will not assist you."

Her eyes hardened. "Fine. Then we'll stop them without you."

She hurled him towards Mr. White's forcefield. Mid-flight, Mr. White snapped his fingers. Mateo spasmed, clutching his abdomen, curling into a ball as invisible pain wracked him. He slammed into the energy shield and crumpled at Mr. White's feet.

James led the charge against the Apex-controlled Reapers. Andrea, Sofia, Liam, and Robert followed.

The Evolved Thinker focused its assault on the other Taken.

Meanwhile, Jess, Isaac, Brian, and Emily stood firm, firing at the advancing Pallid.

Mateo lay gasping in shallow breaths, while Mr. White loomed above him like an executioner.

Sofia struck the Reapers using a series of kicks and punches.

Andrea used psychokinesis to throw bodies aside.

James zoomed above, firing energy beams, as Robert's NanoSword morphed into a massive warhammer that crushed the Taken with each blow.

The Hunter streaked alongside Liam, the two colliding in a blur of blades and fists. They traded blows at a breakneck pace, each strike echoing across the chamber.

Nearby, Fyre locked into brutal combat with the Evolved Thinker while Aion slipped unseen through the melee. In a flash, she seized Robert, hurling him against the wall with bone-cracking force. He crumpled to the floor.

"Robby!" James streaked toward him. Jess broke from the firefight and sprinted to his side.

He took Robert's hand and helped him to his feet. "You okay?!"

Robert nodded, breathing hard. "Yeah. The suit took most of it."

Jessica steadied him with a hand on his back; eyes locked on Aion.

James caught her look. "I'll handle her. Return to the others."

Jess gave a sharp nod, then spun away, Ice Pistols flashing as she cut a path through the Pallid.

Robert turned toward Liam's clash with the yellow Taken. "Over here!"

Liam shifted the fight in their direction. As the Hunter closed in, James seized it by the throat and slammed it to the ground. Robert summoned his NanoWarhammer and struck the Taken's skull.

Liam wiped sweat from his brow. "I had that under control."

James grinned. "We know, buddy."

His expression hardened as he pointed past the melee. Aion was slipping through the mass of blue Taken, closing in on Sofia and Andrea.

James gestured in a circle with his finger. "Protect them. Double team the Apex after we clear the Reapers."

Robert and Liam nodded. Liam slipped out his MicroKnives and sprinted toward the fray.

James launched himself at Aion, but the black Taken darted aside at the last instant. Robert shifted his NanoWarhammer into twin MicroAxes and carved through the blue Taken at his father's flank. Liam knifed his way along the edge, each thrust punctuated with a grin and a whispered, "Stab."

James landed, squaring off with Aion. They charged one another. She slid under his right hook and drove a knee into his gut. Aion struck his back with both fists, causing him to fall to the ground. Before he could recover, she kicked him repeatedly in the ribs, each strike a blur. James gasped for air as Aion raised her foot over his head, then froze mid-motion, limbs jerking.

Andrea, her hands trembling but firm, held the Apex aloft with psychokinesis. She shot a look at her daughter. "Now, Sofia!"

Sofia summoned twin orbs of blazing energy, merged them into a single sphere, and thrust it forward. The blast hit Aion in a searing flash that lit the entire chamber. Blinded, everyone shielded their eyes as she crashed to the floor with a sickening thud.

Fyre roared, her voice shaking the walls. "No!"

She snapped the Evolved Thinker's neck in one brutal twist, then rushed to Aion's side. Hauling her partner upright, Fyre dragged her toward Mr. White's forcefield. A section opened, and they entered.

As Emily's vision cleared, her stomach dropped.

The Pallid's appearance had changed.

Their pale flesh now burned an angry red, and one appeared much closer than before the flash. Too close.

Emily spun to her father. "Help!"

Brian charged and tackled it into the wall. They hit hard, his gun discharging in the scramble. The monster collapsed on top of him. He shoved it off. Emily smiled in relief until she saw his hand clamp over the bite on his neck.

Blood welled between his fingers, spreading across the floor beneath his head.

"Dad!" Emily's voice cracked as she and Liam rushed to him.

Mr. White trembled with fury. "Look what you've done, Mateo."

Mateo coughed, forcing out the words. "Stop... dodging responsibility... for your own actions."

He wheezed, his speech ragged. "This is the result... of you betraying me."

Mr. White dropped a section of his forcefield and strode out. He yanked Mateo up by the collar and smashed a fist across his face. Blood sprayed from Mateo's mouth and nose. Mr. White let him crumble, then turned his gaze on Brian.

Flanked by Fyre, he advanced. His hands snapped outward, fingers splayed.

Every Pallid and Taken in the chamber, except the Apexes, lifted roaring into the air. Mr. White clenched his fists. In an instant, they crumbled to ash. The remains sifted down like black snow.

James whirled, chest tightening. *'How do we stop that level of power?'* he thought.

Mr. White dropped to his knees, clutching his skull, unleashing a tortured wail. Fyre moved to steady him, but he waved her back. Staggering upright, he pressed on toward Brian.

Liam flinched, eyes wide.

Mr. White kneeled beside his sibling. "I'm so sorry this happened to you. If Mateo hadn't brought the Taken and Pallid here, none of this would've occurred."

Brian smiled, squeezing his hand. "It's your fault too... but I forgive you. I just wish I'd had more opportunities to know my brother."

A tear slipped down Mr. White's cheek. "Me too. I'm sorry... for everything."

He staggered and looked at Emily.

She eyed him. "Can't you do anything?"

Mr. White shook his head. "There's not enough time."

Emily clutched Brian's other hand. "Don't leave me, Dad."

He smiled. "I'll never leave you. I will always be with you."

Tears streamed down her face. "I'm sorry I left. I wasted so much time we should've spent together."

Brian brushed her tears away with trembling fingers. "And I regret going on that mission."

Turning his head, he fixed his gaze on Liam. "Take care of her."

Liam nodded, eyes burning. Brian breathed quick, ragged breaths until he stopped moving.

Liam picked up Brian's gun and placed it against his temple.

Emily stared at Liam. "Please don't do it."

He put his hand on her shoulder. "You don't want him to come back as a Pallid. Look away."

She turned around and flinched as a gunshot pierced the silence.

Emily fell to her knees and cried harder.

Liam kneeled and hugged her.

Across the room, Andrea stood over Mateo. Her voice broke. "Was this worth it? Worth losing your daughter, your wife... your life?"

Mateo shook his head weakly. "We should've taken Sofia and left the city. I should have listened to you."

Tears slid down her face. "Yeah... you should've."

Black hands clamped around Andrea's throat. Aion hoisted her into the air, one grip at her neck and the other at her legs.

Behind the group, Fyre seized Isaac's throat and lifted him.

Liam let go of Emily and locked eyes with Fyre. With a yell, he sprinted at her. At the same moment, Sofia hurled herself at Aion.

Mr. White thrust out both hands, halting them mid-charge. Liam dangled on his right, Sofia on his left. She kicked and thrashed, watching her mother choke. He glared down at Fyre, his eyes burning with fury.

James powered up while Robert and Jess leveled their weapons at Mr. White, waiting.

He shook his head slowly. "You might not get my actions or reasons, but trust that I don't intend any harm. I wish to save you. Join me, and I will save you. Stand in my way, and I will have to go through you."

Liam shouted, his voice cracking with rage. "All you do is talk! Again, you beg us to join you, and every time we answer no. Even as your brother lies dead, you threaten his best friend and Sofia's mom. Now you claim you're saving us, but from what? You never tell us from what!"

An alarm erupted, shrill and relentless. The signal swept through The Agency, flashing red lights throughout the area pulsed.

A systematic countdown began. "Ten minutes remaining."

Within the forcefield, the two large machines activated and began operating.

A white circle of energy spun between them, growing in intensity and luminosity with each passing second.

Mr. White gestured toward the timer, his expression grim. "I'm trying to save you from what occurs when the clock reaches zero."

Emily raised her weapon, her voice shaking. "What happens then?"

Mr. White's mouth tightened. "Everyone inside this dome dies."

Chapter Seventeen

James glared at Mr. White, the red alarm lights flickering across his face. "What do you mean *'Everybody inside the dome dies'*?"

Mr. White exhaled through his nose, almost weary. "What did you expect? That we'd let Mateo march Taken around the globe? The Reapers alone can convert thousands in days. Within a week, every nation would collapse. There are also the Pallid."

He looked at a pile of ash that used to be Pallid and Taken. "Do you know who created them? Where did they originate? Imagine both species loose beyond the forcefield. It would be catastrophic. Hard choices had to be made."

James's voice hardened. "What did you do?"

Mr. White drew in a deep breath, steady and deliberate. "We're dropping a nuclear bomb into the dome."

Everyone gasped.

He exhaled through his nose. "The forcefield will contain and amplify the blast, ensuring nothing, Taken, Pallid, or otherwise, survives."

Energy crackled in James's palm, a sphere of blue light forming. "What gives you the right to decide that millions of people in Allegheny should die?"

Mr. White chuckled, muted but cold. "That decision wasn't mine, though I agree with it entirely. The President issued the final order."

Jess stepped forward, shaking her head. "Why would she do this?"

Mr. White turned his gaze on her, voice calm and unwavering. "Why wouldn't she? Strip away the emotions, and the answer is obvious. You always sacrifice millions of lives... to save billions."

The words hung in the air.

No one moved. Nobody breathed.

Only the countdown, relentless and mechanical, ticked through the silence.

Mr. White's gaze swept over them. "Everyone here understands sacrifice. You've risked yourselves for each other repeatedly these past few days. It was possible to leave on the first night of the outbreak, but you remained. You came back for Mateo. And then, you tried to stop me."

He pointed toward the countdown, its numbers burning red. "Time's running out. Join me. Follow me. Or stay here and die."

Suspended in the air under Mr. White's control, Liam glared at Fyre, who still gripped his father by the throat.

"Hey, up here." Liam called. "For the last time, we won't join you. We came to stop you."

Mr. White met his gaze, calm and unshaken. "When will you learn? There is no stopping me."

Aion snapped Andrea's back across her knee with a sickening crack. She crumpled beside Mateo, eyes wide, mouth frozen in shock. His trembling hand reached for hers.

Sofia ignited in fury, energy flaring around her as she screamed and strained against Mr. White's invisible hold.

He shook his head. "You're not going anywhere."

With a flick, he hurled her left, smashing her through wall after wall. Aion strode to his right, ready at his side.

Robert's NanoCape shifted, forming a NanoHammer. He flung it straight at Mr. White.

Without looking, Mr. White caught it midair. His lips curved in the faintest smile. "You can't defeat me with my own weapons."

Mr. White threw the weapon back at him. Robert's remaining cape morphed into a shield on his arm, but the impact still launched him through several walls.

Mr. White slammed Liam to the ground twice, then flung him against the wall to his right. "You will join me."

Liam landed hard, bloody and disoriented. Emily fired two shots, but Mr. White swatted the bullets aside with a flick of his hand.

Fyre screamed, clutching her arm, and dropped Isaac before sprinting toward Mr. White's left. Isaac collapsed to his knees; hands pressed to his stomach. Emily's gasp caught in her throat; she rushed to him, applying pressure to the seeping wound.

Jess fired in full-auto mode with her Ice Pistols. Mr. White deflected the rounds to his right, then seized her in the air. "Resistance is futile."

James formed a massive ball of energy and hurled it at him. Fyre and Aion leaped in front, absorbing the blast. The force slammed all three into the machines, breaking Mr. White's hold on Jess. She plummeted. James caught her in his arms.

He glanced at the others. "Check on everybody."

Then he turned back to Mr. White, eyes blazing. "I'll finish this."

Aion charged. James feinted a right hook, baiting her. As she ducked low for a knee strike, he grabbed Aion's leg and hurled her across the room into the far-left wall.

Fyre ran at him with blistering Hunter speed. James tracked the blur, snared her throat during her lunge, but Aion recovered fast, sweeping James's legs out from under him. He released Fyre as he crashed to the floor.

From the ragged hole in the wall, Sofia burst forward, a ball of energy in her hands. Aion ducked under her fists and snatched her legs mid-flight, slamming her chest into the ground. She rolled onto her back, only for Aion to pounce, raining punches into her midsection.

Robert's NanoHammer smashed into Aion's face, knocking her a few feet away.

Sofia gagged and rolled to her side, spitting blood.

Above her, Mr. White extended his hand, and his psychokinetic grip yanked James into the air.

Mr. White stared at James. "You are not the hero here. I am. You're just too blind to see it."

He slammed James into the ground. Pain rippled through him, and his vision blurred.

Mr. White hauled him up again. "Join me, and the suffering stops."

Another slam. James's nose burst, blood running down as dizziness took hold.

Mr. White leaned close, eyes cold. "Have you learned the lesson yet?"

He drove him into the floor once more. James lay gasping, every breath ragged, the taste of iron filling his mouth.

Mr. White and the Apexes turned toward the machine.

James remained motionless for a few moments. Just the shallow rise and fall of his chest. Then he pushed himself onto his knees. His arms trembled. He planted one foot, then the other, swaying but upright.

Mr. White glanced back. "Still playing the hero?"

He hurled James into the ceiling. James crashed down again, then gathered the last flicker of strength to launch himself forward.

Mr. White caught him mid-flight and flung him through multiple walls, each impact shuddering the structure.

Mr. White grabbed his head and fell to his knees.

James smashed through a third wall and hit with a bone-jarring thud. He lay staring at the ceiling as debris crashed on him, lungs clawing for air. Then everything went black.

Fyre and Aion hauled Mr. White upright. He cast a glance at where James broke through the first wall. "This time, stay down… before you get yourself killed."

They steered him back toward the machine. With their support, he stepped into the forcefield and began adjusting the controls.

Jessica and Robert ran to the holes in the wall and picked their way through the wreckage.

James floated in an endless void. The silence pressed heavily against him. He tried to move, but his body felt paralyzed.

He glanced around for Robby and Jess but didn't find them. Then a light appeared.

A soft blue glow flickered in the distance, pulsing like a heartbeat. It swelled, expanded, and drew closer until it enveloped him.

Within it, a presence leaned closer.

Warm lips brushed his, and for an instant he felt alive and whole.

His pain and exhaustion burned away.

But the light shrank, slipping from his grasp. It receded, leaving only darkness… until the void faded, and the fractured ceiling of the real world came into view.

James gasped and rolled onto his side, blood spilling from his mouth.

Jessica and Robert dropped to their knees beside him, eyes shining with tears.

She cradled his battered face. "Thank God."

Her voice trembled. "Jamie, you need to stand. Six minutes until the nuke hits Allegheny."

James forced himself upright and swayed on his feet.

Jess seized one of his hands. "I've got you."

Robby clutched the other, and pulled him steady. He clutched James, refusing to let go. "I thought he'd killed you."

Jessica joined the hug. "So did I."

James wiped the blood from his mouth. His gaze drifted through the jagged holes his body created. "If he wanted us dead, we wouldn't be breathing. He murdered the General. Why not finish the job and kill everyone?"

He tried to step forward but faltered. Jess and Robert slid beneath his arms, bracing him, and together the three pressed toward Mr. White.

James glanced to the side. Liam kneeled over Isaac, Emily clutching him from behind, her tears soaking his back. "I'm so sorry," she sobbed. "I was trying to hit Mr. White."

Liam's fists tightened as he stared at his father's lifeless body, tears cutting down his face.

Nearby, Sofia kneeled, watching as her parents clutched each other's hands. Andrea's voice broke as she met her daughter's eyes. "I can't feel my legs, Sofi."

James pressed on toward the forcefield.

Robert and Jessica steadied him on either side.

Emily rose with Liam and guided him to join them.

Jess lifted Sofia to her feet, and together the battered survivors advanced as one.

Mr. White turned to meet them, his expression carved from stone. "Are you finished with these pointless interruptions, or shall I finish you to prove that nothing will stop my mission?"

James raised a trembling hand, pointing at the fallen General. "Why didn't you kill us; like you killed him?"

Mr. White sighed. "From the moment you stepped through that door, I told you I was acting for the greater good. That I wanted to protect your families and your friends. I asked you to help me save the world and told you that in the end you'd side with me. Has the fact that I spared your lives opened your eyes? If not... they'll close forever in five minutes."

Liam pointed to Isaac. "You didn't spare his life."

Mr. White shook his head. "No. But I did not fire that shot. Killing him was never my intention. I respected your father. The only necessary death was Mateo. General Johnson died because of his disloyalty. Isaac and Brian should not have perished."

He turned his gaze to James. "I'm going into that portal. On the other side, an opportunity awaits. If you follow me, you'll see. If you stay here, you will die. Furious as you are now, you will thank me when you arrive. The choice is yours, either life or death."

James glanced at them.

Sofia and Liam were battered and bloodied.

Emily's face was pale with fear.

Robert's eyes locked on Mr. White.

Jess tapped two fingers against her wrist to remind him of the time.

'My main job is to protect them. I can't do that if we're all dead.' he thought.

His gaze ended on Liam. Liam gave a single nod.

James turned back. "We'll join you if you can defeat us one more time. If we win, you're going to use all your resources to help us fix this, our way."

Mr. White smiled. "If that's what it takes."

Fyre and Aion surged forward, but Andrea threw out her hands, halting them mid-stride. They roared, thrashing against her grip. She screamed, straining to keep them at bay.

James rocketed at Mr. White, one arm extended, the other coiled with swirling energy. Mr. White raised a hand and shoved him back with invisible force. As James hurtled away, Liam blurred past, smashing a fist into Mr. White's jaw. Sofia followed, pelting him with twin bursts of energy. Before he could repel her, Robert's NanoHammer slammed into his gut. Mr. White doubled over just as James returned, driving a charged uppercut into his chin. The blow launched him skyward before he crashed to the floor with a heavy thud.

Andrea screamed and lost her grip. Fyre and Aion broke free, charging straight for James. Jess fired, her freezing rounds locking them in layers of ice until their movements slowed to a crawl. James and Sofia unleashed a joint blast, shattering the ice and blasting the Apexes backward. They landed in a heap beside Mr. White.

He staggered to his feet, blood spilling from his nose and mouth, his black suit disheveled.

Fyre and Aion rose to his side.

Mr. White readied himself to attack.

From the ground, Mateo laughed.

Mr. White glanced at the countdown: three minutes left. His eyes snapped to Mateo. "What do you find so funny?"

Mateo drew a rattling breath. "That you ever thought you'd win."

Mr. White's jaw tightened. "I know I can."

Mateo coughed, the sound wet and raw. "I'm about to die because of you. When I do... my followers will set the Taken loose across the world."

Mr. White glared at him. "You're bluffing."

Mateo turned his head and smiled at Mr. White. "I have scientists worldwide who see me as a god. They've aided me from the beginning through encrypted networks. I gave them the formula, and they have bred their own Reapers, Thinkers, and Hunters in their cities and continents.

My one order to them was that in the event of my death, which you made sure of, they are to release their Taken. They believe in my vision. My followers will obey. When my Deadswitch triggers, the Taken shall flood the Earth. So, I win... and you lose. Even if you defeated them all, you've already failed."

Mr. White straightened his tie, blood still on his mouth. "A minor inconvenience. In the end, I always prevail."

Mateo stared at the ceiling. "Not this time."

He exhaled, eyes drifting shut.

Mr. White looked at James and the others. "This... situation is all my fault. The terrorist attack, the Taken, not foreseeing the Pallid. It's on me. I wanted to protect the world. And instead, I've doomed it."

James glanced at the countdown. Two minutes left.

Mr. White pointed at him. "We will fix this together, and we'll do it your way. I'll see you... where the grass is greener. Walk through the next portal and thank me later."

He turned and stepped into the portal with Fyre and Aion. The rift sealed, then reopened. The forcefield collapsed, exposing the swirling circle of white light.

Sofia kneeled by Mateo, checked his pulse, then met Andrea's eyes. She shook her head.

Sofia kissed her father's forehead. "Goodbye, Papa."

She lifted her mother into her arms and rose to her feet. The others turned to James.

Liam gripped his shoulder. "Do you think he truly wants to save the world our way?"

James kept his vision on the countdown. One minute remained. "I don't know what his intentions are, but I know ours. We have to leave now."

Liam nodded.

Sofia glanced at the portal. "We don't even know where it leads."

James grimaced. "True. But staying means death. That portal could be a chance to fix everything."

She shuddered with her exhale. James stepped into the swirling circle of white light with Jess and Robert. Sofia carried her mother through after him. Liam and Emily cast a last look at their fathers, then followed.

The timer flashed down to three seconds... two... one. Zero.

The dome opened as an A.I.-piloted plane swept overhead.

A bomb fell as the forcefield sealed itself, streaking toward Mateo's lab on the North Side of Allegheny.

****

The Agency shook. Mateo's eyes snapped open. He gasped for breath, searching the room. It was empty.

With a grimace, he rolled onto his stomach. His right arm clawed forward, dragging his wounded body as his left clutched his abdomen. The electromagnetic pulse carved a path for the destruction to spread through the dome.

He staggered to his feet long enough to slam the activation button, then collapsed on his back. A portal bloomed before him, its white light churning.

Outside, the nuke obliterated people, Taken, Pallid, cars, and entire blocks of buildings. Fire and radiation poured through the city. Debris rained from the ceiling as flames and fallout screamed down the elevator shaft.

Mateo rolled to his belly and inched toward the light. Death surged down the Agency's halls.

A slab of the roof crashed onto his legs, pinning him two feet short. He clawed at the floor, dragging himself inch by inch. One foot away.

Mateo stretched his arm, fingers trembling near the portal...then the world went dark.

Chapter Eighteen

The kiss of the morning sun, and soft lips, woke James. He opened his eyes to find Jess smiling down at him.

James was in black cotton pajama pants, shirtless. She wore a lilac short set patterned with flowers.

He sat up. "Where are we?"

Tears slipped down her cheeks. "This looks like our apartment... but how did we get here?"

James looked around. The tall white dresser stood with their photo on top, framed in silver beside her jewelry stand. The little trinkets she loved were right where she always left them. In the corner sat her oversized red reading chair, its cushions still indented from the hours she'd spent curled there. Above the bed hung a black and white painting of a lion and lioness.

He smiled. "We're home. I'd say this is impossible, but I would've said the same about the Taken, superpowers, the Pallid, and portals a few days ago."

James shook his head. "Being back here might be the least weird thing yet."

He exited the bed and then proceeded toward the window.

His breath caught. '*What the hell?*' He thought.

James beckoned. "Jess, come look at this."

She hurried to his side. "What is it?"

He pointed to the skyline. "Sure doesn't appear like a nuke just hit the city."

She nodded. "Yeah. There's no destruction anywhere, and everything looks better than it did three days ago."

James swept his gaze from left to right. "Is it me, or is the shopping district bigger? The buildings seem taller."

Jess pressed closer to the glass, scanning the view. "It's not you. There are flying vehicles... plus everything seems cleaner."

He turned to her, brow furrowed. "What's happening?"

She shook her head. "I don't know, Jamie."

Jessica looked at him. "How do you feel?"

James glanced down at himself, then gave a half-smile. "Not like I almost died last night."

He sank back onto the bed, exhaling.

She settled beside him and kissed him. "I don't know about any of this, but I know we're alive and together. That's enough for me right now. I want to savor every second we get."

They held each other's gaze, both smiling through the strangeness. Then Jess's HoloWatch chimed from the nightstand. She reached over to grab it, then stopped cold.

James sat upright. "What is it?"

Her eyes glistened as she looked from the watch to him. "It's Tasha."

He blinked at the glowing caller image. Brown skin, short hair, and the same grin that he'd seen a thousand times. "But... you told me she died."

Jess's voice trembled. "She did... in my arms."

Her hand shook as she accepted the call. "Hello?"

A projection shimmered above the watch. Tasha's face, clear and alive, smiling as if nothing had happened. "Hey, y'all. Jess, why are you crying?"

Jessica wiped the tears away from her cheeks. "I'm just so happy to see you."

Tasha smiled. "Aww. That's sweet. Here I thought you were still emotional because he popped the question last night."

Jess and James froze, exchanging a wide-eyed look.

James's voice came out tight. "Tasha... what's the date?"

She chuckled. "Today is Christmas Day."

His throat tightened. "What year?"

She laughed, shaking her head. "Y'all must've celebrated a lot if you can't remember that. It's 2047. Well, at least for six more days."

Jessica gasped and clapped a hand over her mouth, her eyes brimming.

Tasha frowned. "Jess, what's wrong?"

Jessica swallowed hard, forcing a wobbling smile. "Nothing is wrong. Everything's perfect, Tash. Just... let me call you later, okay?"

Tasha softened. "All right. Bye girl."

The hologram blinked out, silencing the room.

Jess turned to James, her hands trembling. "When I saw the flying vehicles, I thought he sent the group to the future, but he took us back in time."

He shook his head in disbelief, his chest heaving. "That's...that's impossible."

She checked her HoloWatch again as if it might disagree with Tasha, but the glowing numbers were clear. December 25th, 2047. Her voice cracked. "Two years. He sent us into the past two years."

James dragged a hand down his face, the weight of it hitting him all at once. "Why a couple of years and not three days? Or a year to stop the bombing? He didn't have to send us this far."

Jessica's lip quivered as she whispered, "Unless... he wanted us here."

James shuddered. "That's not a good thing. Without knowing what he'll alter, we can't tell if things will end up the same, better, or worse."

She looked out the window. "At first glance, things seem improved, but appearances can be deceiving."

He studied the skyline again. "Would he stop the Taken and the Pallid from ever existing? Is everything going to be repeated? Or... is something even more terrible coming?"

Jess gazed at him. "What could be worse than what we just experienced?"

James stared at her. "I don't know, but it terrifies me."

Robby knocked at the door, cutting through James' thoughts. "Can I come in?"

She slipped on her robe.

James pulled a shirt over his head. "Come in, buddy."

Robert entered wearing his favorite navy anime pajama set and rushed into their arms. They held each other tight.

He looked up at his dad. "How are we back in our apartment? I thought the bomb destroyed the county."

James managed a faint smile. "Well..."

Before he could say more, his HoloWatch buzzed to life. The glow lit his face as he leaned over the bed to answer it. His eyes widened.

'Of course. Why didn't I think of this sooner?' The realization hit him like a jolt.

A familiar face appeared above James's watch.

Caramel skin, warm brown eyes, and straight shoulder-length hair. "Hey, James. Where's Robby?"

Robert scrambled across the bed. "Mom?"

Candace beamed. "Hi, Robby! When are you coming over today? I want to celebrate the holiday with you too."

She studied him more closely. "Why are you crying?"

Robert shook his head. "I'm not. Superheroes don't cry."

Candace chuckled. "Oh, you're a superhero now?"

James chuckled. "Too many HoloGames. I'll bring him early this afternoon."

She nodded. "Okay. See you then. Bye, Robby. I love you."

Robert smiled. "Love you too, Mom."

Her hologram dissolved into the air.

Robby turned to his father, and his brow furrowed. "What's happening?"

James set a hand on his shoulder. "Mr. White sent us back two years."

Robert's eyes widened. "How did he do that?"

James exchanged a glance with Jess. "We don't know. But it looks like he has changed some events that happened. Just look at the shopping district; it's different."

Robert rushed to the window and pressed his face to the glass. "Whoa. It's bigger than before."

He spun back toward them. "What do you think he's trying to change?"

James counted on his fingers. "I can imagine a few things he might try to prevent. The attempts on the President, Colonel Brian's original death, the Lemon Station bombing, and his dealings with Mateo."

Jess stared at him. "What else could he change?"

He shook his head. "Everything."

Robert grinned. "I don't care what he changed or changes. I got my mom back."

James put a hand on his son's shoulder. "You sure do. Make the most of this second chance."

Robby nodded and headed toward the door. He paused in the doorway and frowned. "I can't find my suit, Dad."

James furrowed his brow. "Since we traveled into the past, maybe it didn't come with us. For all we know, they hadn't created it yet."

Robert sighed. "I want it. Being in it helped me with my anxiety. I was filled with determination and felt I could do anything."

James crossed the room and hugged him. "Why do you think that was?"

Robby tapped his dad's shoulder with a playful punch. "Because it made me a superhero, like you."

James laughed. "Well, I saw how brave you were, and I couldn't let you outdo me."

They all chuckled until the doorbell rang.

Jess jumped to her feet. "I'll get it."

Jessica tied her robe as she left the bedroom and headed to the front door. Jess glanced at the camera and broke into a smile.

Opening the door, she exclaimed, "Hi, Sofia!"

Sofia smiled back. "Hey… Jess."

They embraced before Sofia cleared her throat. "It feels strange being back in time, before everything happened. I woke up at my parents' house this morning. When I realized where he'd sent me, I was happy. The sight of my mom and dad, as I remembered them, made me cry."

Jessica nodded. "I did the same thing when my friend Tasha called me. She died in the Lemon Station bombing. And Robby, he cried when his mother called."

Sofia's smile dimmed. "Why would he send us to the past?"

Jess shrugged. "We think he's trying to change things. But landing on December 25th, 2047… it feels like a gift."

Sofia let out a short laugh. "It sure does. Did Christmas bring anything amazing for you?"

Jess's eyes brightened. "Yeah. At midnight in 2047, James proposed to me."

She held out her hand, the ring catching the morning light.

Sofia tried to match her smile but couldn't hide the flicker of pain. "That's... fantastic. You'll relive the engagement again."

Jessica shook her head. "Been there, done that. I got kidnapped, and lost time with Jamie. We're not wasting another second. James and I are getting married A.S.A.P. A small ceremony, with family and friends."

She tapped Sofia's arm playfully.

Sofia rubbed the spot, her voice warm but softer now. "Congratulations, Jess. I'm sure it's going to be beautiful."

Jessica grabbed Sofia's hands. "You're invited if you want to come, of course. Just tell me what you think afterwards."

James walked into the living room, dressed in blue jeans and a red V-neck shirt with a black lion head across the chest. He grinned when he saw her. "Sofia."

She smiled back as he pulled her into a big hug. For an instant, her chest tightened.

Sofia glanced at Jess. "Mind if I borrow him for a moment?"

Jessica nodded. "Of course. See you later."

"Bye." Sofia gave a small wave as she and James headed down the hall. They passed the GravLift and took the stairs to the lobby.

He glanced around. "The last time I came down here with Rob, Reapers attacked. People died, including the women who became Fyre and Aion."

His eyes lingered on the walls, as if he could still see the bloodstains. He shook his head. "We might have to move if we're going to make this second chance count."

Sofia cleared her throat. "How's Robby?"

James managed a grin. "Handling all this well. The best part of being here is that he has his mom with him again."

She smiled. "That's huge. I'm glad for him."

Sofia hesitated, her voice catching. "I called Lydia as I came here. Talking to her after watching her die three days ago was…surreal. But having her back is worth every second of weirdness. Stranger was speaking with my parents. After everything I learned, especially about my dad, it'll be hard to see them the same way. I am mostly happy things are back to normal."

James nodded. "I understand. Once you learn more details, it's difficult to ignore new truths."

He smiled. "How are they though?"

She chuckled. "My mom remembers everything, and she can walk. The injury doesn't seem to affect her. Papa seems to be who I remember. When I mentioned Mr. White, he didn't know who he was."

James grinned. "Maybe that's best for the world, and your dad."

They exited the stairwell, crossed the lobby, and left the building. Sofia and James sat on a bench out front.

She took James's hands in hers. "Our brief time together was nice, everything considered. I wish the situation were different, but the love of your life came back to you, and I can't compete with that. At the cabin, I told Robert I would protect you, even from yourself."

Sofia smiled. "She seems wonderful. I won't hurt her, although I wanted you. She doesn't deserve that."

Sofia jabbed him playfully. "But we'd better stay friends, or I'll fight you."

He laughed. "Of course we will."

James squeezed her hands. "I was also eager to start a relationship with you. Realizing she was alive, it upended my life. I can't pass up this opportunity for a second chance. She doesn't deserve that, and I couldn't hurt her."

He smiled at her. "We were friends before the Taken, and we still are after what we went through together. No matter what happens, you can count on me."

She kissed him on the cheek and hugged him.

Liam pulled up in his S.U.V., climbed out, and walked over. He embraced Sofia, then James, and smacked James on the shoulder with a grin. "So, what's next, boss?"

James glanced at them. "We try to protect the world however possible. Sofia will watch her dad, who seems to be his old self. We work to defend people against Mr. White and any threats. If he turns, we stop him again."

Liam chuckled. "If that happens, stopping him may be tougher than you think this time."

He flicked his HoloWatch, projecting a news article above it. "Mr. White is now Vice President."

James stared at the headline. "How far back did he go?"

Sofia looked at him. "He must've returned to at least 2043 to run with the President."

James gazed at them. "What else has he changed in four years?"

Liam shuddered. "I'm sure we'll find out."

James shook his head. "Even though he holds the VP title, we saw his true nature, plus his capabilities."

He turned to Liam. "How are your father, Brian, and Emily?"

Liam smiled. "My old man's alive. I've never held him for as long as I did today. He shoved me off, grumbling that I was playing a prank. So yeah, same cranky elderly dad. None the wiser about anything."

They all laughed. Liam exhaled. "Emily and Brian visited this morning. She and I talked a lot since our dads are oblivious. Before he died, my father admitted he wished he didn't know I had powers. I guess he got his wish."

He pointed at James and Sofia. "Speaking of which, did either of you try to use yours?"

They both shook their heads.

Liam sighed. "I tried. They're gone."

Sofia frowned. "What do you mean, gone?"

He clenched his fists, frustration written all over his face. Then, without warning, he sprinted down the sidewalk. His sneakers pounded against the pavement, much slower than his Super Speed. When he stopped, his chest was heaving, and sweat already beaded on his brow.

"I mean," he said hoarsely, "they're not here anymore. My speed, it's gone."

Silence hung between them.

Liam looked down at his feet as if they belonged to someone else. "When I ran before, the world blurred. I felt... unstoppable. Now I'm back to a forty-yard dash that couldn't beat a middle school track star. Do you know what that's like? To lose the one thing that made you extraordinary?"

Sofia and James held out their hands and tried to ignite their powers. Nothing happened. They attempted again, straining to power up, but still nothing.

Liam stopped in front of them, keeling over, out of breath. "How do we save the continents and defend them from Vice President White with no abilities?"

James sighed. "We'll find a way. Just because circumstances changed, doesn't mean we shouldn't try. Yes, it'll be harder, but life isn't easy. Hard goals are worth the effort."

Liam and Sofia nodded.

James smiled at them. "As long as we work together, I'll take our odds against anyone. With or without powers."

Liam threw a few punches. "Yeah. We'll whoop the world's ass."

Sofia snickered. "The bad guys in the world, you mean."

He stopped mid-punch. "Of course that's what I meant. Did you think I was talking about little elderly ladies who jaywalk?"

James and Sofia laughed.

Liam pulled James into a hug. "Well, I'm heading back to the old man and my new lady."

James patted his arm. "Congratulations, Liam. Take care of them. We'll all have to get together soon."

Liam smirked. "Of course. I'm going to watch over them like a guardian angel."

Sofia chuckled. "Liam, can you give me a ride?"

"Sure," he said with a nod. "I've got something to run by you on the way."

Liam looked at James. "I'll hit your Holo tomorrow."

She hugged James. "Thanks for believing in our team, and in what we can do together, even if our powers are gone."

He smiled. "We accomplished a lot for two people with no experience. Now that we have it, the only thing that can stop this group is ourselves."

She pointed to her HoloWatch. "I'm gonna call you in the morning."

James waved. "Talk to you then."

She slid into Liam's S.U.V. He glanced at her as the engine hummed to life. "So, I've been thinking about team names. Tell me what you think of these."

The vehicle pulled away from the curb.

***

Later that night, Jess and James curled up on the couch watching their favorite comedy movie on HoloVision.

She burst into laughter at the scene that always made them cackle.

When he didn't laugh, she paused the film. "What's wrong, Jamie?"

James turned to her. "I've been thinking about how we'll stop Mr. White if it comes to that. I have a few ideas, but without our powers... I don't know how much we're going to matter to him, or in a fight against him."

Jess kissed him, her smile glowing. "Everything will be okay. If anyone can figure this out, it's you. I believe in you. Robert, Liam, Sofia, they all trust you too. Have faith in yourself. Anything's possible."

He grinned. "Thanks, Jess. I'll call it a night.

She glanced at the clock. "It's only ten. Could I convince you to drift off with your head on my lap?"

James chuckled. "Your thighs are comfortable, but the couch isn't. My body's craving the bed."

She kissed him. "Alright. I'll finish the movie and be in later."

He rose and headed toward the bedroom.

Thirty minutes after that, hard knocking rattled the front door. Jess stood startled and checked the camera. Two sleek black boxes sat outside the apartment. No one was in sight. She opened the door, looked both ways, and then pulled the cases inside the apartment.

Someone taped a note across the top:

James,

I told you more than once that I wanted your help to save the world. After some thought, I want Robert and Jessica's aid as well. Any of you can open the containers. See you soon.

Vice President White

P.S. If you're not feeling like yourself, give it time.

Acknowledgements

Out Now!

The Outbreak: The Survive Saga, Book 1

The Evolution: The Survive Saga, Book 2

The Aftermath: The Survive Saga, Book 3

If you enjoyed this book, please leave a review telling others why they should read it. This helps spread the word. Thanks.

Special thanks to the following people: Tina, Miyah, Sammy, Mom, Daniel, Noelle, Zuri, Rue, Dianne, Donald, Sandy, Marsha, Shawndre, Drew M., Lindsey, Wendy, Drew W., Maddi, Rod, Phil, Kim, Jocelyn, Justin, Dawn, Deb, David, Precious, Jeremy, Lamont, Jason and ZeppelinDG.

She pressed her thumbs to the scanners. The locks clicked, the lids lifted, and her jaw dropped. Heart racing, she bolted down the hall.

Jess entered the main bedroom and froze. "Wake up Jamie!"

James opened his eyes, and he fell onto the bed.

He frowned. "What just happened?"

Jess grinned. "You were floating."

James sat upright. "I was?"

She nodded. He stretched out his hand, willing the energy to come. Blue light swirled around his body, brighter and more intense than before they used the portal.

A laugh burst from him. "My powers are back! And they're stronger. Like there's more inside me than ever. How is that even possible?"

Jessica shook her head. "I don't know. But you need to see what Mr. White sent us."

She pulled him into the living room. From her case, he lifted the sleek Echo bodysuit, with the twin Ice Pistols nestled beneath it. He crossed to Robert's box and uncovered the gleaming Warlock armor. Jess handed him the folded note. James read it in silence, absorbing the words.

He met her gaze. "So... do you want to save the world with me?"

Jess leaped into his arms, legs wrapping around his waist, and kissed him hard. "Of course I do."

***

The office was dim, its soft wood walls swallowing sound. A single open door loomed behind them, while the wide observation window stretched across the front like the eye of a vault, showing a dark and empty area.

Vice President White sat at his black mahogany desk; his gaze fixed on Madam President Mary Jackson and his recruit. They sat in two of the four seats. He lifted a sleek black case and flicked it open. Inside were ten glass vials that gleamed, the liquid pulsing as if alive. "The power to safeguard the United Continents of America is right here."

President Jackson frowned. "Or the potential for another disaster."

Vice President White gave a measured nod. "Not this time. I have rewritten every protocol. Daily psych evaluations. New fail-safes. The team secured Project 1939 more tightly than any prior program. I've had four years to plan what happens next."

Her lips pressed into a thin line. "All your scheming better work this time. This mission aims to protect the world, not doom it."

Mr. White closed the case and slid it into his bag, his jaw tightening. "I failed my reality in The Cascade. This time, I will not lose."

He rose to his feet. "Madam President—"

The words died in his throat as the air beyond the glass rippled, then tore open with a blinding surge of white light. The circular portal spun as Mr. White's lips curled into a smile. "Ah. Our guests are here."

For a moment, the light roared, empty. Then two silhouettes stepped through, the brilliance fading to show their forms. They walked through the door and sat in the pair of vacant seats.

Vice President White spread his arms as if welcoming destiny itself. "Now... it begins."

He turned to his recruit. "Bring them up to speed."

Mateo's grin widened. "With pleasure."

THE END...FOR NOW.